One Wild Summer!

by

Mick Fee

This book is a work of fiction. Names, characters, businesses, organizations, places, events, and incidents are the product of the authors' imagination or are used fictitiously. Any resemblance to actual persons, living or dead, events, or locales is entirely coincidental.

Library of Congress Catalog Card Number:
Pending

ISBN-13: 978-1499150650
ISBN-10: 1499150652

This book is dedicated with love and gratitude to Dot and Leo Fee, my parents, who long-suffered through my 30 years of summer lifeguarding, all the time wondering when I would "grow up."

And, to all of those terrific personalities with whom I had the great pleasure and privilege to have known and worked with during those thirty years of "sitting wood."

Foreword
(Oh, those) Wildwood Days   Bobby Rydell

Years ago, openly talking about all of the "inside stuff" that follows in this narrative may have been seen as a betrayal to the cult of ocean lifeguarding, but in reality, these "tricks of the trade" belong to a different age in America--one that was freewheeling and sexually liberated. Therefore, these happenings are more reminiscences than revelations.

Also, you may find this novel to have been written a bit helter-skelter, but that just how *this* summer at the beach evolved, with many, many episodes tumbling, one after the other, from Memorial Day weekend through to Labor Day Monday of 1976. Just imagine yourself privy to a summer full of fun, watching these wild guys carry on, as they did with total license and abandon. Unlike most other novels, it's not so important that you keep track of all of the characters, and there are a good few *characters,* to be sure. Since, if you were on your beach chair or in a bar having a beer, you wouldn't have to know their names to enjoy watching their antics.

"Do you know that there has
        never been a rape in this town?
    Well, that's because you can't
        rape the willing."-
    Dorothy Tier,
        long-time South Jersey Resident.

In the summer of '76 the movie, *Lifeguard: Every Girl's Summer Dream* came out, and, it opened in the ocean-side, beach resort town of Wildwood, New Jersey to great fanfare. With it, a dozen of Wildwood's finest and tannest uniformed, real lifeguards delivered the reel of the film to *the Shore Theater* on the boardwalk. In *Lifeguard,* Sam Elliott plays 32-year-old California lifeguard, Rick Carlson. Rick has two troubling dilemmas, and these form the movie's major plot: first, whether to give up lifeguarding to make some real dough as a *Porsche* salesman, and, the other is having to decide between two women. Most inveterate summer ocean lifeguards face the same sorts of dilemmas, only with slight variations. The first similarity happens to them twice a year, once when the summer ends and, friends and family ask, "What are you going to do now?" and, then again with the advent of summer when they ask incredulously, "You're not going back to the beach again, are you?" So, seasoned guards do identify with Rick in experiencing career pressure.

On the other hand, these Jersey lifeguards found it greatly amusing and a rather unrealistic portrayal of a lifeguard, in that Rick had only two females on the line. On the beach in Wildwood this would have amounted to a seriously-flawed summer.

1

A few years ago, one of the Wildwood guards had been given the nickname Denny McClain because at summer's end he and the Detroit Tigers' Denny McClain had closed out the season with the same number of wins--thirty-one.

Lifeguards delivering the movie reels for the movie *Lifeguard* to the Shore Theater on the boardwalk in Wildwood, New Jersey. They are from left to right: Allen Czyszko, Tom Griffin, Bobby Love, Peter "Gull" Salo, Gene Reidy, Jimmy "Snuffy" Singer, Larry Fee, and Jimmy McManus.

Many thanks to the Wildwood Historical Society for the use of this photo.

Book 1: May
Friday, May 23, 2014,
  the start of Memorial Day weekend
The Boys Are Back in Town **Thin Lizzy**

"Yeah, kid, you're gonna think that I made a lot of this up, but as far as I can recall it's all true," the old-timer said. "Back then, the lifeguards of this beach patrol liked to say that, 'Every day of the 100-plus days of summer we did something that would have made the front page of a small-town newspaper.' (Today, it'd no doubt be reported in *USA Today*.) I'll just tell you about one summer, that of 1976, since it really sticks out in my mind as a really wild one. Amusingly, though, kid" he continued, "lifeguards were subject to a sort of self-imposed secrecy about what went on 'last summer at the beach.' Although no rule governed our tacit agreement, common sense enforced this compact, since if these stories were related to a lifeguard's winter buddies, they'd say--or at least think-- that he was full of it.

"What has to be kept in mind is that these events were a product of the 60s and 70s, the interval between 'the pill' and 'the AIDS epidemic.' These were wild times for youthful society at large, but for some inexplicable reason, lifeguards have always had license to go beyond the normal cultural boundaries. And, as you will see, the characters of this story took an exponential leap beyond the 'normal boundaries.'"

Friday, May 21st, 1976
Wasted Days and Wasted Nights
   Freddy Fender
      Before heading east to the Jersey *Shore,*
Walter Finley, aka, Walt "the Salt" and Bill
Hennessy, aka, "Dollar Bill" had stopped at their
favorite watering hole in Denver, the *Bull & Bush
Tavern* for a few pops and to say goodbye to the
staff, bartenders and waitresses, before getting in the
Chevy for the eighteen-hundred mile drive back to
the Shore. "Are you boys really driving nonstop back
to New Joysey?" Robbie their main bartender asked,
emphasizing the "Joysey." "Yeah, Robman," Walt
told him, "it's about eighteen hundred miles, and
with a few stops for a little grub, gas, and a few six-
packs, we should make it back in thirty-six hours or
so." "Well, good luck, lads, and, here, have another
one on the house."
      In short order, a fifteen-minute stop turned
into an hour and a half, and "one for the road" into
half a dozen. By the time the Beach Boys' cassette,
Endless Summer began its three-month encore in
Walt's Chevy, the lads were pretty blasted. On their
drive through busy downtown Denver, the business
district, Dollar Bill was yelling out the window,
"Hey, straighten your tie. How ya gonna make any
money that way!" Luckily, green lights opened all
the gates and there were no real confrontations with
some of the highly-irritated business types.

6

Last summer...

On most South Jersey beach patrols the official minimum age for lifeguarding applicants is eighteen, but if a kid is big enough, knows how to swim well, and/or is *connected,* this requirement may be modified down to sixteen, or even fifteen. Last year, Charley Booth, who at the time was seventeen and going to be a senior in high school after that summer, looked to be about twenty-one or so. In fact, the senior guys got to calling him "Babe," owing to his hulking size *and* his remarkable resemblance to a young Babe Ruth.

With the drinking age at eighteen, he rarely even got "carded." While in the bars at night, he typically had to create some fiction that would pass with the older girls that he routinely met. One night, out at the *Martinique Lounge* he made the acquaintance of twenty-four-year-old Mary Lou Ryan and the two really hit it off, dancing and drinking together for hours. Toward "last call," Charley suggested they continue the party over at his apartment. They were there in a few minutes and spent that first night and the remaining nights of Mary Lou's week-long vacation in bed together.

Fortunately for Charley there existed at *the Shore* an atmosphere in which serious questions were seldom asked. For instance, most summer friends rarely knew each other's last names. Charley's creative resume consisted of, "I'll be a sophomore at Villanova in the fall, and I haven't made up my mind yet as to a major." This ploy successfully skirted any pointed references to physic, chemistry, math, or the like. Mary Lou's time at *the Shore* went by blissfully, spending every night with Charley, however, they ran out of time all too quickly. Afterward, though, she was able, to get down for a few weekends before having to gear up for the coming school year.

Charley thoroughly enjoyed the remainder of his first year "on the wood," that is, on the lifeguard stand, but Labor Day Monday and the school bell on Tuesday signaled a completely different life. Lost in reveries of "the beach," Charley somehow found room 16-A, and mindlessly took a seat at a vacant desk. The starting bell jolted him back to reality, but not half as much as his being singled out by name by the teacher. *How could this be!* But, it *was* none other than senior homeroom teacher, Miss Mary Lou Ryan. As she indicated that Charley step out into the hallway, Charley desperately tried to awaken from this bad dream, but there was no escape. Making sure that no one was within earshot, Miss Ryan said, "Nothing happened this summer. Right?" Charley looked her straight in the eyes and replied, "I have no idea what you're talking about."

By November of the school year, Charley's final year of high school, Miss Ryan began to feel somewhat confident that her accidental secret with Charley would be kept. Throughout the year Charley, now a senior, had played his role of "total stranger" exceedingly well, never giving the slightest intimation that teacher and student had "met" prior to beginning classes this year. Charley turned eighteen in April, a fact of which Miss Ryan was cognizant from his student records. And, as May came 'round, heralding the advent of yet another summer, Miss Ryan found a quiet, private moment to ask Charley, "What are you doing for the summer, Charley?" With a gleam in his eye, he responded, "I'm lifeguarding again in Wildwood by the Sea. What about you, Miss Ryan?" Nonchalantly, she offered, "Oh, I just might get down this summer to the beach in Wildwood to say 'Hello,'" never in the least giving away her eagerness at the thought of their getting together again.

Sunday, May 23rd
Can't Get It Out of My Head
Electric Light Orchestra

Somewhere in Kansas, at a sprawling truck stop, returning Wildwood lifeguards Walt "the Salt" and "Dollar" Bill made another concession to summer "Hey, Walt, check this out!" Dollar Bill said, pointing to one of the shelves on which sat a small, dusty bottle of *Coppertone.* We *gotta* buy it. We can sniff it from time to time along the way and think about *the Shore* and all the fun that we're going to have this summer." They didn't need to know about the embryonic connection between the sense of smell and emotional memory stored in the limbic system of the brain; nonetheless, with one whiff of the magical cream and with the Beach Boys' *The Warmth of the Sun* as background, the pair experienced a flood of wonderfully amorphous memories. Another product that had this strong evocative power with the lifeguards was *Noxzema.*

9

So many guards had been with lots beach honeys who had gotten a bit too much sun, that *Noxzema*, too, had this profound reminiscent effect. *Just let me rub a little of this on you, honey. It'll really help.* And, with a little imaginative memory, those white strap-marks on a honey's sunburned back would magically reappear.

Back for another summer…

Sexual freedom formed the "spirit of the age," in the late sixties and the seventies. And, on stand # 9 sat two of its chief exponents. (Note: For a list of the lifeguards of this story and their stand assignments please go to the very last page of this book.) Clem and Ryan, aka, "Dunes," wintered as lifeguards in Florida's Broward County. South Florida and the northeast resorts on the Atlantic Ocean have exactly opposite tourist seasons. The two lads had been making the twelve-hundred mile drive for several years now. During the winter months, with air and water temperatures mild and comfortable, towns from Fort Lauderdale to Miami would have many migratory lifeguards in their employ from lots of Jersey beach patrols.

Ryan, originally from Baltimore, who in his senior year at the University of Maryland, College Park had gone south on spring break to Fort Lauderdale and got a look at beach life and liked what he saw. Having been on the swim team in college, he had little trouble passing the Lauderdale Beach Patrol swim test that fall after he graduated with his degree in history. A tall sandy-haired guy with a pleasant manner, he hit it off with everyone in

10

Florida. Among his new friends was fellow lifeguard, Clem, who brought him up to Wildwood by the Sea to become a summer ocean lifeguard.

That's the Way I Like It
KC and the Sunshine Band

Clem "the Clam," whose moniker derived not from the mollusk, but rather from the "species" termed the "bearded clam." Clem had a penchant for one sexual specialty. Among the boys, a favorite line of Clem's was, "You just haven't made love until you come out of it with your face looking like a glazed donut!" Another boast of his was, "If you aren't licking it, I'll steal her." He claimed that there were times when in bed with a girl he'd completely forgotten about coitis, or that there were times when the girl would tap him on the head and ask him to come up and do her.

Clem did discriminate, though. He would go through his preliminary routine, just as a golfer might go through a stepwise process before teeing off. Clem would get the honey in bed, begin by kissing, and in the process gradually remove his and her clothes. After some fingering to get the honey wet and in the mood, Clem would surreptitiously bring the fingering hand up to her breast that he had now come down to fondle with his tongue. With nose and finger together, Clem would make his decision. Only with great disappointment would Clem settle for screwing. Another favorite of Clem's was his corruption of the banal seventies saying, "My place or yours?" He turned it into, "My face or yours?" Sadly, years later, Clem never got over the

11

invention of panty-liners, as they concealed what lay behind a snug bikini bottom. Clem liked to hold up his right hand, with his thumb and index finger held close together, and with his fingertips aligned, forming a nice approximation of a vulva, and say, "This is what those goddamn panty liners are hiding."

The Summer of 1976

These were sexually explicit times, the seventies. Very often, a lifeguard, after discerning that a young nymph was of the liberated sort, he would ask her right there on the beach, "Hey Darlin,' what do you like to do in bed? Do you like to do sixty-nine?" or "Are you on *the pill* or do you use a diaphragm?" Questions that would, no doubt, be outrageous today. Or, it would occasionally happen that after stopping a honey to chat, the lifeguard would ask her what she was doing that night, to which she might reply, "I hope I'm doing you tonight." "I think that we could arrange that," was the usual reply. So, with these sexual informalities discussed, there'd be very few surprise and usually no disappointments that night. Some guards would even put a sock in their nylon tank suit, knowing that the bulge wouldn't go unnoticed by the wilder sort of girls, and, so, the apparently big, big "package" served as bait to attract the more libidinous ladies walking the beach.

Another variation on this theme would be a beach honey, who when asked by two lifeguard stand partners, "Are you seeing a lifeguard tonight?" she might reply "I can't make up my mind, they're all so cute." "Well, maybe you don't have to," the guard would reply, "Would you like to get together with a few of us tonight? If you pick out the ones you like, I can get them together over at my place right after the beach." If the honey agreed to it, this would be the reason for an impromptu drinking "train" party. Usually a half-dozen of the guards would be organized, and in between beers, one of the lads would go into the bedroom and have his fun with her. Back then, this would have fallen into the category of what people would refer to as "sport fucking." And, as such, the participants were on an equal footing. Among the guards, it was tacitly agreed that the ladies always be treated gentlemanly. Often, afterward, the glassy-eyed honey might say something to the effect of, "I have never had this much fun before in my life." Ironically, the same honey might go back to her hometown and tell dates, "I don't go all the way." So often, once a girl crossed over that causeway into Wildwood by the Sea, everything changed. No neighbors, no relatives, no witnesses.

Just like rock stars, the lifeguards had their "groupies." One clever Wildwood lifeguard in a house with four other Wildwood lifeguards had concocted a plan to capitalize on the groupie phenomenon. He had talked his fellow lifeguard roommates into kicking in and making up dozens of red tee-shirts with white lettering, the sparse script of which was to be just the number. "317," this being the numerical address of their five-bedroom summer house. Seeing lots of these 317 tee-shirts around town, very few summer people really got to learn the significance of the number, which created a sort of secret society. But, when one female wearer of the 317 shirt espied another girl wearing it, too, she knew that the other "317" had *also* done all of the Wildwood lifeguards living at 317 East Glenwood Avenue.

Memorial Day weekend,
May 28th to the 31st, 1976

As springtime would come 'round again, groups of guys and groups of girls would get together and make pilgrimages to the Jersey *Shore* to look at a few of the many advertised apartments, decide on one, and put deposits on their summer digs. On the calendar, Memorial Day weekend kicks off the summer, and the beach crowds can be huge, with hordes of city dwellers anxious for summer to finally begin again. Once summer does get going, lots of them would spend their two-week vacation at *the Shore* and then maybe their summer weekends, too, if they didn't live too far away. So, because their time to have fun was so brief, relative to the whole year, there attached to their stays at *the Shore* a great deal of urgency to live it up. And, although the lifeguards of Wildwood *did* have more than a hundred days of summer to work with, they, too, operated with the same sense of urgency, and, especially so as the number of days of summer began to grow shorter. Given this big push to have fun, lifeguards routinely entertained young ladies who would say, "I'm nothing like this at home." And, this was absolutely true. Often a lifeguard would have sex with a girl who had never even had it with her "steady" at home.

After Memorial Day weekend and for the first few weeks of June, the city of Wildwood will employ its returning veteran guards only on Saturdays and Sundays, due to the light crowds and the tight budget. Until the middle of June, town would be pretty quiet, with not much to do at night for the lifeguards who had come back early in the summer, so there were few opportunities for them to meet honeys on the beach. Out at the bars at night, an off-the-beach lifeguard was just another guy in the bar promoting himself and trying to persuade some girl to go home with him.

Book 2: June
Saturday, June 5ᵗʰ, 1976
Let's Do It Again   **the Beach Boys**

Last summer, Clem the Clam, the South Florida winter lifeguard had fallen into a routine of from time to time knocking on Julie's door after the bars had closed. Often reluctantly, she would let him in and in a very short while, the two would be having a high time in the bed. What with how dull these early June nights were, Clem took a chance and went around to the apartment where Julie had stayed last summer. A bit alarmed to see Clem so early in both the summer and in the evening, she smiled and gave him a tentative hug. "Hi, Honey, how have you been? You know, in the mad dash to get out of town and back to South Florida to lifeguard down there, I somehow lost your winter address and phone number. How about getting together tonight?" Clem enthused.

But, now, this early in the summer, Julie knew that her bargaining power had greatly increased and said, "Sure, let's go out to dinner." Clem, who, in South Florida was a bit of a devotee of the thoroughbred race track subscribed to the railbird wisdom that you never feed a horse before the race, that is, unless you want the horse to bag the race. Clem had actually spent whole summers without ever taking a girl to dinner, saw the spot he was in, and, with faked enthusiasm said, "Sure, I'll pick you up at eight." In two weeks or so, when things at *the Shore* got cookin' again, Clem was confident that he'd get the old arrangement back and that this

16

dinner with Julie was, after all, just an investment in the future.

Friday, June 11th

By the time the Denver boys, Rob, aka, *Osprey,* and Brian blew into Wildwood apartment pickings were slim. They had hoped to go in with some guards who hadn't yet filled out a big house, but this summer they were out of luck there. Eventually, they had to settle for a three-bedroom above the *Fisherman's Inn Bar*, a local hangout way back on a deep-water canal populated by commercial clammers and fishing boats. The *Wurlitzer* jukebox had everything from Glenn Miller to the Rolling Stones, but whatever played and at whatever hour the music was loud. But, the boys were stuck for a place to stay and, due to the undesirability of the location, the price was right, too.

The *Fisherman's Inn* had its regulars, all of whom stood out as characters. By some sort of drunken protocol, each of them had their own regular stool at the bar. Stanley, the cranky old bartender, worked just about every hour that the bar was open. As the season got going and the lifeguards upstairs settled in, he got especially ruffled when the boys, after a particularly rough night out at the bars, would pop down before work and order a couple vodkas on the rocks and a couple dozen clams on the half shell, which, of course, Stanley, as the bar's only employee, had to shuck. On seeing the lads in the bar partaking so early, the regulars would ask, "Off today, fellas?" "Yeah, were off today and we're going crabbing." These occasional morning stops

17

before work would take the edge off the hangover and jump-start yet another great day of working the beach.

Saturday, June 12th, 1976,
Wildwood by the Sea, South Jersey
Only the Strong Survive   Jerry Butler

'Not a day for a swim in the ocean, a gloomy day; nonetheless, at the water's edge of this summer resort town stand 127 shivering, anxious, young aspirants. Most of the dread comes from the thought of swimming a half-mile in this frigid, 52-degree water. All have come in hopes of securing one of the scant 14 summer ocean lifeguard jobs available. Most of the 127, with a few stragglers showing up a bit late, have been briefed on the details. Most of the young men there are aware of just how few openings there are. And, they have been told that those who finish high enough in the order will be probably be offered the chance to attend two weeks of "rookie school," which will run from nine in the morning until one in the afternoon, Monday through Friday. They will receive half a day's pay for the four afternoon hours, when they will sit the lifeguard stand (known in inner circles as "the wood") with a seasoned, experienced lifeguard.

Straightforward as the test will be, in that the first fourteen out of the water are usually invited to rookie school, it's not an equally fair one, in that the top swimmers may not get the job. That's because some of the aspirants will have the benefit of some privy information, the main kernel of which is knowing how glorious a summer "on the wood" can

18

be in this topsy-turvy, mostly blue-collar carnival town. Most guys in life may fall in love once or twice in their lives and perhaps marry one of these loves. As a summer ocean lifeguard, however, one has the opportunity to be infatuated by a different honey every week. Superficial as this may sound, it's a real emotional treat to those young men who do get to experience an endlessly romantic summer. With this in mind, and probably having been schooled by friends who are already on the squad from summers before, several less talented applicants will fight their way into the succeeding, top of the pack. Undaunted, they will brave the icy water, ever-mindful of the envisioned reward lies ahead.

How the lads are dressed for the swim serves as another advantage/disadvantage. Ideally, the optimum outfit is a tiny speedo tank suit, a pair of swim goggles, and a double layer of swim caps. Yet there will be a lot of tyros who, in the interest of modesty, will have donned walking shorts (called "Bermuda shorts" back then) complete with pockets that fill with water and act as what a competitive swimmer would call a "drag suit."

Outside of the cloudy, wind-swept beach conditions, the lads will have the small advantage today's relatively calm ocean. The one-foot wave sets should present no problem for the entry. Ears perk up at the, "Swimmers take your mark" command. And, then the long-protracted bleat of the *Acme Thunderer* whistle from Lieutenant Joe Shelly, who then turned to Captain Capacio and said, "Now we'll see who really wants this job." "You know,

Joe," the captain said, "I've been giving this test for over 25 years and I'm convinced that if it were easier, say, with warmer ocean temperatures, we wouldn't get the right kind of guys on the patrol. That it's so formidable a test shows that the boys who pass it have grit. Real determination. They could easily make more money at McDonald's than working the beach, but they go through this ordeal to become ocean lifeguards. That really tells you something about their character. They're a special lot."

For a capable swimmer, in favorable conditions, the half-mile out and back swim should take about ten to fifteen minutes. Today, though, it took just two to three minutes for the field to be reduced by a third. With that frigid splash of the briny on their pale bodies and with teeth chattering, forty or so who began the tryout summarily decided that it just wasn't worth it. Now the real test began. As the minutes ticked off a few more here and there turned back, no doubt alarmed at their inability to take a normal deep breath in the chilled water. Some, for fear of them drowning, were pulled into the lifeboats that were there for just that purpose. Others who quit the swim on the way out were able to make the short distance to shore on their own.

At the fifteen-minute mark, the cream slowly began to emerge and stumble to their feet in waist-deep water, most of them shivering uncontrollably. As had been agreed upon, the first fourteen were told to come up to beach headquarters for hot showers and then to report an hour later, at 10 a.m. to fill out their work forms. Several of the lads who finished out of the top fourteen were offered the opportunity to become "alternates," which meant that if they liked, they could come back as often as they chose to check on whether a spot might have opened up. Back in 1966, the oft'times narrator of this story, Alfie Henderson came in fifteenth and did go back twice a day during the ensuing days of the next week, and did eventually get on the patrol, some two weeks after the tryout and two weeks after rookie school. But, that's a tale for another time.

In just a month or so, the water will warm up to nearly (and sometimes even higher than) eighty degrees. With that, and just the luck of an average summer season, there will be endless days of what ocean lifeguards call "postcard days," days of perfect blue skies and warm seas. The crowds will come and the beach will look something like this...

Saturday, June 12th
Sister Golden Hair   **America**

Yesterday, a rather precocious beach nymph named Anne came up to young Charley Booth's stand # 11. She had a magnificent body, standing about five-foot four, with fulsome breasts that were alluringly revealed by her scanty pink bikini top. With big blue eyes, long blonde hair, youthfully pulled back into a ponytail, and having a very perky demeanor, both Charley and his stand partner, "Seadog," Gary Lieber, were on the edge of their seats the moment she stopped by their stand.

Pointedly, Anne asked the kid "What do you do to have fun at night in this town?" From her forward-leaning body language she made it clear that she really wanted to be with Charley that night. By now, Charley had become accustomed to getting good receptions from females on the beach, but to date, it had never been *this* easy. "Well, you and I could get together right after the beach and have some real fun," Charley offered. "I'd really like that. In fact," she giggled and said, "You know, I think all three of us could have a really good time together," looking flirtatiously at Seadog, who did have his suspicions about her having said that she was eighteen, but was seriously tempted nonetheless. "Charley, at seventeen, you have little to worry about, but perhaps I do," Gary said in an aside to Charley.

Despite his trepidation, Gary did go along with the idea. He and Charley picked Anne up at six-thirty and brought her to Gary's digs. Gary coached

23

Charley, "OK, kid, you go in the bedroom and get it started." In no time the clothes were off and they were going at like mad, in the missionary position. Subtly, Gary came into the room wearing just his boxer shorts. He took his position on the bed, lying right next to the enthusiastic couple. Through the fly of his shorts, he directed Anne's hand to his stiffy and automatically she began a vigorous hand-job, her strokes keeping time with Charley's penetrations. Eventually, though, Charley began to run out of steam and slow down. Simultaneously, Anne's hand motion flagged in rhythm with this reduced tempo. Sizing up the situation, Gary immediately said, "Yo, Charley, pick it up, pal. You're letting me down." The teamwork had momentarily fallen apart. But, Charley quickly responded, "OK, Seadog," and once again it was, *Full speed ahead, Captain!*

Where the Boys Are   Connie Frances

Earlier in the spring four young ladies, Jan, Miriam, Betsy and Mary, had become friends over the course of their freshman year at Slippery Rock University. All four hailed from western Pennsylvania, with Miriam being the only one actually a resident of this college town of 3000-plus. During the school year, they had hatched a plan to spend the summer at the Jersey *Shore.* A few of their coed classmates were lucky enough to have spent last summer there, had a glorious time, and brought back lots of juicy stories. A summer of absolute freedom and sunshine, and, perhaps a love affair or two, as well. *Every girl's summer dream.*

24

Back in February, over Presidents' Day weekend, Jan and Betsy drove the 400-plus mile trip to *the Shore* and found a four-bedroom place right in the heart of Wildwood by the Sea, so that everyone would have their own room. Split four ways, the rent was rather inexpensive. Before agreeing to the rental terms, the landlady and owner, Mrs. Dunn, had reminded them, "Now, no wild parties or loud music." "Oh, no, Mrs. Dunn, we aren't that kind of girls," Betsy impressed upon her. And, the deal was made. The lease ran from Memorial Day weekend 'til and including the second weekend in September, since, lots of summer residents like to eke out that last bit of summer, before surrendering to winter. Often, weekends at the beach are still somewhat populated into the fall when remarkably the weather can be the best of the whole year.

As is usually the case with attractive people gravitating toward each other, all four of the Slippery Rock coeds, Jan, Miriam, Betsy and Mary. were, in their own way, quite fetching. But, that's where the similarity ended. Jan, a cheerleader for football and basketball, had the most out-going personality, a trait that would benefit all four of the girls in the coming summer. Mary had almost gone in on a place at *the Shore* the previous summer but had been too slow in committing, and when she did her spot had been already taken. So, as she told the other girls, "I'm really anxious to make up for lost time. I know this summer is going to be a great time!" The other three of the quartet would probably describe Betsy as "boy crazy," a description that fit her perfectly. When the

25

subject of the upcoming summer at *the Shore* was discussed, all Betsy could say was, "All those good-looking boys!" Miriam, the most diffident of the four, was also the most serious one of them, holding a perfect 4.0 GPA in her first year in an as-yet-to-be determined major. Before being convinced, she had said to the other girls, "Are you sure you think it's a good idea for me to go in with you on a summer place at *the Shore*? I don't really know if I'll fit in." "Oh, of course you will," they reassured her, all the while knowing that it would be a social experiment, one that the all three hoped would succeed.

Sunday, June 13th

A slow night so far for Rob. None of the ladies he had invited to the *Terminal Bar* had shown up, and he didn't have his travelling partner, Brian, who made an early date with this doll he had met at the beach who was down by herself and "looking to have some fun." Fortunately, for Rob, the "Osprey," there was still the *Beat-the-Clock* at the *Fairview,* it being Monday night. But, there the three hours 'til midnight had whizzed by and now Rob had a snootful, and still no girl. Finally, at two, he sent himself home.

When he got back to their place, from the bedroom he heard Brian and "the doll" talking, no doubt in between bouts. Poking his head in, he saw from her bare shoulders up what an absolute cutie Brian had found. Emboldened by the booze, he asked, "Hey, Brian, can I do your girl?" Taking no offence whatsoever, Brian simply said, "It's up to Amanda." Amanda smiled broadly, and Brian excused himself to go get a beer, only to return a half-hour later. Though not a very common occurrence, this sort friendly accommodation does reflect just how sexually loose the sixties and seventies were.

The next day was their day off so that morning they went downstairs to the *Fisherman's Inn Bar* and primed the pump with a couple vodkas on the rocks, with a splash of club soda, telling cranky Stanley, the bartender, "We don't want them too cold and we don't want them too bubbly." Leaving the bar, they passed through the hallway of the adjoining apartments. Abruptly, Osprey asked Brian, "Do you hear that?" As they paused to listen, they heard a melodic girl's voice coming from the community bathroom. Following the singing, they peeked in through the partially opened door, and saw a buxom red head immersed in the bathtub. The few soap bubbles left a clear view of her flaming red pubic hairs. "Hi, I'm Osprey and this is Brian," the lads introduced themselves. And, without so much as blinking an eye, she replied, "Oh, Hi, I'm Susan." Osprey politely inquired, "Susan, you sure have some magnificent titties. Would you like me to lather them up for you?" Her demure smile and just the slightest blush of her fair cheeks gave the answer. Then, with Osprey massaging Susan's nice big, pink nipples to erection, Brian gently slipped his finger into her pie. Susan became ecstatic, but, after ten minutes or so, the boys got a little antsy and announced that, "We have to go." Susan just couldn't believe that these guys didn't want to stay

27

around and follow up on their bathtub foreplay. Passing out on to the street, Osprey looked at Brian and they both just broke up. Brian summed it up with, "You know, Rob, we could have stayed and had a lot of fun with that girl, but there's a lot more fun for us out there today. Let's get to the beach."

Seasons in the Sun   **Terry Jacks**

Wildwood by the Sea, the seaside resort town where this tale takes place is unique in that it has a very lively two-mile boardwalk and 105 bars, and that's in a town that's just about two and a half miles long by a half a mile wide. Its sleepy winter population of five thousand swells to well over a quarter of a million at peak times during summer months. Wildwood is geographically formed by one of the dozens of barrier islands that comprise the 127 miles of New Jersey ocean coastline, affectionately call *the Jersey Shore*, or, simply, *the Shore* by its beach devotees. *The Shore* spans from Sandy Hook to the north, to its southernmost reach at Cape May Point. These ribbon-like islands have been the locus of summer fun for generations of vacationers. Traditionally, Memorial Day Weekend signals the official start of summer at *the Shore,* with its conclusion abruptly punctuated by Labor Day Monday, when most East Coast schools and colleges returning to activity the next day, Tuesday.

Wildwood shares its six-mile island with two other resort towns, Wildwood Crest to the south and North Wildwood to the north, each manned by their own autonomous beach patrols. On a sunny summer weekend the head count on the entire island amounts to nearly half a million. Some old-timers compare summers here to Coney Island in its heyday, back in the 1920s. A carnival town with an ocean-side beach. Lots of other nearby ocean resorts, with their million-dollar summer houses, have a very dignified air about them, whereas, Wildwood's summer tourist are mostly blue-collar types from inner-city towns like Philly, Allentown, Pittsburgh, and Baltimore. Working-class folks bent on having a high time during their once a year, one or two-week vacation.

It's from these sorts of families that future lifeguards come. Young sons see the fun and the pretty girls fawning over the lifeguards, and it's in the craw of their prepubescent minds to get that job for the summer *when I get old enough.* In contrast, in the posher resort towns you'll find that the ocean lifeguards are typically the 15- to 18-year-old sons of the summer property owners. In Wildwood there are no parents bringing lunch to the stand and hovering over their wards with ever-watchful eyes. To the contrary, the younger lifeguards of our story have become freer than they have ever been, with a temporary release from hometown and parental constraints. Once the young man passes the swim and rescue tests and rookie school a senior guard becomes his stand partner and mentor, a tradition that has gone on for over 100 years.

Wildwood by the Sea is but 25 streets long, each running from beach to bay, and every one populated literally by dozens and dozens of apartment buildings--two, three, and four story wood-frame houses closely crammed into every available space. Thirteen moveable, wooden lifeguard stands, towering some seven-feet aloft and manned by two and sometimes three lifeguards, protect the huge crowds of ocean frolickers that spill out of these creaky old rooming houses.

The author, Mick Fee, on the job in 1976.

Monday afternoon, June 14th

From four hundred yards away, 11-year lifeguard, Alfie Henderson, could see the beach patrol jeep making its stops at lifeguard stands, on its way north to introduce and drop off rookies to the senior guards that were getting one. Alfie's stand, # 7, sat in the middle of the two and a half mile, thirteen lifeguard stands on the beach. "Oh, well," Alfie thought to himself, *Let's see what sort of rookie I'll get this year.* Although Captain Capacio and his lieutenant tried to match rookie and experienced guard harmoniously, it didn't always flow as planned. So it was with a bit of trepidation that Alfie watched the baptismal ceremony. In his 11 years on the wood, Alfie had been rather lucky with the rookies with whom he had been assigned.

Ideally, two senior guards who got along well and were pals to begin with would ask to be partners, but that wasn't always possible, as the experience had to be spread out along the beach and there was the responsibility of the one-on-one training that was essential to the continuity of the patrol. Alfie all but knew he'd have a rookie this summer. Which rookie, though, was just a matter of the luck of the draw. Also, there existed a subtle negative reward system as to the setting up of the partners. Well-regarded guards, like Alfie, were usually counted on to train a rookie, whereas, if a certain guard was thought to be a little flakey, he would probably get to sit with a veteran guard with whom he got along and in whom the brass had more confidence.

As the rookie got off the jeep at stand # 7 with very few belongings, Cap and Lt. Shelly introduced Alfie to him as, Jeff Connor. After offering a handshake, Jeff climbed up the rungs of the stand and introduced himself as Jeff Connor, from West Chester, PA, where he was going to be a junior in college come next fall. For the next two weeks, Jeff would be spending the four afternoon hours after rookie training on the wood with Alfie. He appeared to be a sharp kid, but with a bit of humility about him, as well. Alfie like him almost immediately, but had learned in his 11 years of lifeguarding that since he was also Jeff's mentor in teaching the finer rudiments of becoming a good lifeguard, it was best to show a slightly stern façade, at least at the outset. If too much leash is let out in the beginning, it's typically impossible to get it back.

Alfie asked Jeff how the workout went, and got the expected answer, that, "It was hard." For three hours or so each day the lads were run in and out of the ocean on simulated rescues. Jeff also added that at the morning rookie workout at nine, Lt. Shelly had begun his talk to the group by saying to them, "Go home tonight and take a good look in the mirror, because in a very short time as a Wildwood ocean lifeguard, you'll never see that guy again." Very true. Summer as an ocean lifeguard imbued in a young man self-confidence and the ability to make quick and sound decisions. And, rather surprisingly, this personality transformation came about very rapidly. As Rudyard Kipling once put it, "A boy becomes a man when one's required."

The lieutenant then turned to Captain Capacio and asked, "Anything to add, Cap?" "Just this, Joe," Cap began, "Boys, this will be the greatest job you'll ever have. And, the friends you make here will be your friends for your entire life." Although it would take many years in the lives of these young men for the truth of these statements to be tested, every word of it would eventually prove to be absolutely true.

A few days after Jeff was sitting with Alfie, he said that, "I'm really happy that they put me with you. I've heard talk around beach headquarters that you're probably the best all-around lifeguard on the beach." Alfie laughed a little to himself, and, confessed, "You know, Jeff, I hadn't always been the steady, reliable character that I am pretty much now. In my early years, I had been wooed by the nocturnal benefits of the job. In those initial few years, I was out closing the bars every night.

"I remember one of those summers, I got in town without having set up a place to stay for the summer. What I did have, though, was one of those folding alarm clocks in my back pocket, so, every night I'd either get lucky with a new honey and spend the night with her or I'd bump into an old flame and crib in with her for the night. That was some carefree summer, and I travelled light. I used to say, 'If I can't take it into the shower with me, I don't want it.' Day after day, at morning roll call, I'd tell friends, 'No, I'm not going right to the bar after work,' but then I would relent to a few of the boys' cajoling, 'Come on, Alf, stop for one and then you can go look for a place.' When it got into August, and still no fixed place to stay, I thought that perhaps I might take over some guard's place in a house when the guard had to leave the beach early. But, underneath it all, I was really enjoying the challenge. Guards would ask me, 'Where are you sleeping tonight, Alf?' A beach joke. In the end, it became a summer to remember. The whole summer without a place to stay, and with just a travel alarm clock in my back pocket."

Tuesday, June 15th
A misinterpretation…

Today, stand #4 had a bit of rousing excitement, as Harry's rookie, Steve reached for his whistle and said, "Harry, we have to do something about this." Harry intercepted his hand and told him, "Let's just sit on this, unless someone complains. Our job is to just make sure she doesn't drown." In chest-deep, or, rather, breast-deep water was a fulsome honey bobbing up and down, frolicking in the surf, sans her bikini top. Every time a wave would pass it would leave her in the trough, exposing the most beautiful set of titties, glistening in the late afternoon sunshine. Since no one *did* complain, the lads just let nature be, and enjoyed the show, while peering through Harry's 50 power binoculars. Steve's initial reaction had been a conservative one. And, Harry was well acquainted with this sort of Puritanical reaction that some beachgoers have had from time to time. Remarkably, he'd even had

35

complaints from old biddies pointing a scandalized finger at a one- or two-year old toddlers romping on the beach in their birthday suits.

Earlier in the summer, Harry, an eight-year lifeguard, had had a similar bosom treat. One morning when he got to his stand back beach, ready to pull down it down to the waters' edge, there were two lovely blondes lying on their blanket without their bikini tops. Now, it wasn't so unusual to see girls lying facedown without a top, but these ladies were both lying with their nipples pointing skyward. In their lovely German accents, they matter-of-factly asked Harry, "This is OK, ja?" Harry said, "Ladies, it's perfectly fine with me but it's just others might take offence and complain. Then it would become a problem for me, since it might be looked at like I'm not doing my job. The truth is, ladies, that there is probably even a law against it. I really wish you to beautiful ladies could stay here and sunbathe topless all day. But, I'd recommend that if you want to enjoy the beach without your bikini tops on, you take a drive down to the southernmost end of this six-mile island where you'll be alone with the seagulls and a sprinkling of other free-spirited sunbathers, like yourselves."

Wednesday, June 16th
Take It to the Limit   **The Eagles**

At dawn, a few days after classes at Slippery Rock University had ended the four eager coeds, Jan, Miriam, Betsy and Mary, packed the Datsun and zoomed eastward on Route 76, estimating their arrival at *the Shore* to be later that afternoon. The car was abuzz with anticipation. "Do you think we'll meet boys right away?" Betsy gushed. While Miriam, the quiet one, asked, "How long does it take to get there?" For most of the ride, Jan sat quietly in the backseat immersed in Helen Gurley Brown's *Sex and the Single Girl.* With wardrobes consisting of several pairs of shorts, as many tops, a skirt or two, and a sweater and/or sweatshirt for those rare cool nights, they were all set for a summer at *the Shore*.

On the second day there they got several leads on jobs as chambermaids: Chambermaiding offered weak pay but good hours, 7 in the morning and usually done by 3, excellent for both beach time and late-night partying in the bars. Fortunately, there were positions for all four of them at the same huge seaside hotel called the *Oceanview.* Betsy asked, "Will we all be on the same shift?" "There is only one shift," the woman in charge told them, "You may finish at different times. That will depend on when each of you finishes your assigned rooms."

The girls' having but one car posed no problem whatsoever. Every place of interest at *the Shore* was either a walk or a short bike ride. Since the only hills to be found on these barrier-island resorts were the bridges leading to the islands from the mainland, a beach cruiser was all that each of them would need. Simple, they'd just buy used bikes, one-speed clunkers, from one of the many sellers advertised in the local newspaper. All systems go!

A few years ago, before Memorial Day, Alfie Henderson, the lifeguard on stand # 7, drove down to *the Shore* for the summer and a few weeks later his

37

car got a flat tire. Having no pressing need for it, there the car stood until Labor Day weekend. In fact, when he did get around to getting the car going again, mushrooms were growing in the back seat.

Wednesday, June 16th
The Countdown...

Late this afternoon on the beach, Seadog got off his stand and walked back to the coffee shop to use their bathroom. On his return, off about twenty yards of his path back, he noticed a fetching blonde sitting up, while the guy on the blanket with her was apparently asleep, laying facedown. As he briefly glance her way he thought he saw the slightest of waves, but wasn't quite sure. After a few minutes back up on the lifeguard stand again, he turned and looked back in the direction of her blanket. This time, there came a very evident wave. *Hum, what to do?* Encouraged, Seadog turned around several times more. And, each time the gesture became more emphatic. Emboldened, he signaled her to come up to the stand. "Is there any chance that we can get together?" he asked. "Well, tonight I'm going to the Laundromat, so I can get away then," she replied. The tryst was established.

A bit unclear on just how long they had to be together, before she went back to her blanket, he asked her. She simply said, "When the dryer stops spinning, we have to be done." Now, Seadog had experienced sexual time constraints before, but that was way back during high school days when he would sneak in to keep a baby-sitter company, and have to be gone before the kid's parents got home.

38

But, this was something else again. This night, after the beach, the appointment with the blonde *was* kept, but the whole time in bed with her, Seadog couldn't get the dryer's countdown timer out of his mind.

Safe driving…

Although MADD, Mothers Against Drunk Driving wasn't to be established until 1980, public sentiment against driving while intoxicated had been gaining momentum in the years leading up to its organization. Before agreed-upon criteria being established years later, at some blood alcohol level (%), or *BAL,* determinations of drunkenness were left up to the officer when they would stop a car, usually for some other driving violation, like running a stop sign or a tail light out, for instance. So the "system" of culling out the drunks that were on the road ran something like a negative lottery, in other words, you had to be very *unlucky* to get arrested for DUI, "driving under the influence," or, DWI, "driving while intoxicated." Certainly, something had to be done, since, before the stricter enforcement, you'd often hear a guy in the bar say, "Man, I was so drunk last night I don't remember driving home." To which the crowd would often cheer and say, "Buy that man a drink!"

A few years ago, Dollar Bill came up with this lottery's loosing number. After a night out of barhopping in Denver, he was routinely stopped for driving with one of his running lights out. From Bill's slurred speech and the alcohol fumes emanating from the car, the cop knew that Bill had had more than the, "Two or three beers," that Bill had owned up to. At the station Bill blew a 0.256 % (four times the legal limit today) and was promptly given a room, that is, a cell with other kindred spirits for the night. Repeated renditions of *You Are My Sunshine* by the captives did little to lift his spirits.

Once summer returned, Bill took this experience back with him to Wildwood and bought a push bike. Since these small-town resorts became relative ghost towns in the winter, with meager tax bases, they seized the opportunity to raise revenue by setting up sobriety checkpoints, and, went ever further by staking out the late-night bars and hauling in one bar patron after another, none of whom had a prayer of passing the *Breathalyzer* test. Consequently, it became a common to see dozens of bikes parked outside the more popular nightspots in Wildwood. Bill, clever guy that he was, went beyond the then-popular practice of bicycle travel to avoid the DWI. Bill bought himself a tandem bike. And, although he may have looked silly going out to the bars at night with the back seat vacant, he sure didn't when on his way home it was occupied by a cute little honey. After assenting to the offer of a ride home after "last call," the ladies were both mildly shocked but pleasantly amused to see Bill's unconventional mode of transport.

Thursday, June 17th
A Banner Year…

Nineteen seventy-six was a banner year in America. Concurrently, the country celebrated its two-hundred-year birthday and in July the Summer Olympics took place in Montreal, the Games of the

XXI Olympiad, which were especially memorable because of Frank Shorter's winning of the marathon for the first time by an American in 64 years. However, to the guards of the Wildwood Beach Patrol "banner year" had quite a different significance. The "banner" in this case referred to those towed aloft, along the beachfront by single-engine airplanes, bearing messages such as, "Enroll now at Temple U. for your MBA," or "Josephine, will you marry me?" These planes would take off from a tiny commuter airport offshore, and just before liftoff they would snag a loop at the beginning of the banner. The plane's airspeed and the drag on the banner would keep the plane and the banner in contact. Occasionally, lifeguards would hear these antiquated planes sputter over the ocean, which would cause a momentary stall in airspeed and the banner would drop into the ocean below.

Today, the banner that fell to the ocean and was recovered by the Wildwood lifeguards read," Happy 16th Birthday, Tammy." The set reward for the recovery and return of these banners was one-hundred dollars. Typically, in the course of a summer one or two would fall to the ocean. With their eyes trained on the water all day long, Wildwood lifeguards on their stands were usually first to notice the dropped banner and to respond by launching a surfboat with two oarsmen. The standing agreement among the beach patrol lifeguards was that no matter which pair of lifeguards had rowed out and recovered the banner, the reward money would be put on the bar that night and there'd be "drinks around" as long as the kitty lasted. Nineteen seventy-six came to be known as the "banner year" on the beach since there were over ten such nights out at the bars, while drinking beers on the banner reward money.

Saturday, June 19th
Love to Love You, Baby
  Donna Summer
      North of Alfie and Jeff, and about 200 yards away, on stand # 8 sat two veteran guards, Rob, *Osprey,* and Brian. They had been lucky enough to get their request to sit together for another summer granted. *Lucky,* because they already *knew* that they got along and, also, that they wouldn't have to be bothered with training a green rookie. Alfie could see that they were having what lifeguards called a "management problem." Two pairs of honeys stood in front of the boys, on opposite sides of the stand. Even from this distance Alfie could see that all wasn't well. Perhaps their arms folded tightly to their bodies gave the strongest evidence that the ladies were pisssed.

      Right there at stand # 8 it was verbally evident what had happened. The previous night, Rob and Brian had stacked their appointments and in unhappily bad timing, the seven o'clock dates had shown up on the beach at the same time as the ten o'clock girls. It hadn't taken much time for the one pair to realize what had happened. "You bastards! Who do you think you are!" from the seven o'clock dates.

With the "early shift," the lads had invited the ladies over to the house for some margaritas and Jimmy Buffet tunes. The combination had worked nicely. Then, around 9:30 Rob and Brian had contrived a story that they had lifeguard competition in the morning, and had to call it an early night. Now, at the stand it would have been hard to tell which pair of ladies was madder. In just a few minutes, the two pairs of ladies had become allies. "You guys are just two scumbags, and we thought that you were nice guys. Good luck with your perverted lives, you creeps." And, with that the newly acquainted foursome stormed off. Sometimes the juggling act broke down. Oh well, just an occupational hazard. Tonight would be another night, with new prospects and more fun to be had.

Later that night…

Very late tonight, a band of guards from the adjoining beach, Wildwood Crest, surreptitiously made their way under the boardwalk and on to the beach. Their mission, to move the trash cans a hundred yards or so closer to the ocean. Their motive was that their captain, Captain Hobson, had a rule that at day's end when the Wildwood Crest lifeguards knocked off, the lifeguard stands, which from years of annual repainting weighed a couple hundred pounds, must be lugged back through the heavy soft sand to the trash cans. Triumphantly, the guards, after accomplishing their goal, retreated with shouts of, "Who's in charge here, us or the trash men?" After learning of this operation over a few friendly beers, the Wildwood guards had yet another story with which to poke fun at Captain Hobson's beach operation.

A rolling stone gathers no moss
An old proverb

Two pairs of guards on the beach who didn't have a stand, a permanent stand, that is, were Todd, a six-year guard and his rookie, Phil. They were the guys who "covered," manned, that is, a stand when the regular guards had their one day off a week. They were called rovers. They filled in for stands one through seven. Stands eight through thirteen were covered by rovers Ron and Paul, who were both veteran guards. Being a rover had both advantages and disadvantages.

Rovers rarely had "management problems," that is, two pairs of "dates" showing up at the stand at the same time, since they weren't so easily found the next day. On the other hand, when a honey would show up looking for the rover at the stand where she had talked to him the day before it left the rover open to being "snaked." Most fellow guards would direct the cutie to that rover's stand that day, but there were a few cobras working the beach who would say, "Oh, he's off today" or even more effective was, "He went up to college for the week to get some things straightened out." And, then, of course, they'd ask, "What are you doing tonight?" Some guys, not only some guards, didn't get interested in a girl until they saw her with another guy. "Snakes."

Another more innocuous version of getting snaked happened when a guard meets a honey on her first or second day of her one-week vacation and goes out with her all the nights up until Friday. On Saturday, since this guard's city girlfriend is coming down for the weekend, he makes some excuse for not being able to see her again before her vacation ends on Sunday. This opens up the door for other lifeguards nearby who have been seeing her stop at their fellow lifeguard's stand all that week, and who had wished that they had stopped her first when she had just started her vacation. Now, by default, they have their opportunity.

Sunday, June 20th
First I Look at the Purse
The Contours

Clem the Clam and Dunes, had a scheme to compensate for the low pay that working the beach entailed, one that they kept exclusively to themselves. Instead of sending prospects to the *Terminal Bar* for the random nighttime social, they would ask just two girls to meet them, having their own rather secret bar as the rendezvous spot. The bar was the *Keg,* hiding right there in the center of Wildwood. Plastered against the front façade of its building was what appeared to be the gigantic end of a beer barrel, with the door to the *Keg* right where the tap would have been. With just about a dozen bar stools, it was a cozy little haven from the glittering nightclubs that surrounded it. On the taps of this mostly shot-and-beer joint was Larry Magrin, a college wrestling coach at a western Pennsylvania college in the winter.

Tonight the ladies, two working girls from Pittsburgh, down at *the Shore* for a week's vacation

45

showed up at eight, right on time. Clem and Dunes stayed with the Pabst Blue Ribbon and ordered the ladies, a specialty of Larry's, two grasshoppers, made up of equal parts crème de cacao, crème de menthe, and cream. Laden with alcohol, but tasting like mint chocolate chip ice cream, the grasshopper would slide down ever-so-nicely. 'Wow, these are really delicious. What do you call them, again?" they asked. After three of four grasshoppers, the ladies were calling them "lawnmowers."

Now came the time for the histrionics. Clem, making his way to one end of the horseshoe bar, he called Larry the bartender over to play his well-rehearsed bit in the play. Clem would unfold and show Larry a small rectangular piece of paper, Larry would look at it and shake his head "No" and then in a moment "Yes." Upon which, Clem would refold the paper and stow it back in his pocket. Returning to Ryan and the ladies, Clem would explain that Larry said, "I can't cash your paycheck right now but the boss will be in soon and that he will cash it for you." Meanwhile, Clem asked the ladies, "Would you girls mind funding the drinks until the boss comes in." "Oh, what the hell, we're on vacation. Sure, we don't mind at all," they agreed. Needless to say, the boss never did arrive (since there never was one), but after a couple more lawnmowers, er, grasshoppers, the girls didn't care, having the time of their life down at *the Shore.*

Monday, June 21st

After roll call Captain Capacio called Alfie aside to talk over a complaint that he had received toward the end of the previous day at the beach. A middle-aged-sounding woman had called and told this story. She said that the there was a young mother openly breast-feeding her baby "right there on the beach." Apparently, not everyone was into the spirit of "back to nature" of the sixties and seventies.

She went on to say, "When I brought this disgraceful situation to the lifeguard's attention (Alfie in this instance), this lifeguard did nothing about it. In fact, he asked me, 'Where would you have the woman feed her baby?' When I suggested that she could take the baby to the public restroom," the lifeguard replied, 'Madam, would you like to have your lunch in the lavatory?' With this, I immediately saw that there was no further point in talking to this irresponsible lifeguard and called you, the Captain, as soon as I left the beach." After listening to all the details of the incident, Captain Capacio assured the woman that the lifeguard would be reprimanded and he thanked her for the call. Although Captain Capacio didn't relish getting complaints from beachgoers, he and Alfie did have a good laugh about it. Nonetheless, Cap did advise Alfie that in the future he, "Tread a bit more lightly when dealing with the public."

"Days off"...

At the outset of one summer a few years ago, and, after Alfie had been on the patrol a few years, Captain Capacio wanted to do Alfie a favor by giving him his day off on Saturday. On seeing the days-off announcement, Alfie flew into Cap's office to request a change. This perplexed Cap since there were guards who *would* request Saturday or Sundays off. Alfie, however, reasoned that Saturday was the busiest day on the beach, this having two desirable effects: first, it usually was the biggest day for water action, rescues, that is; and, it was also the most interesting day of the beach week, with its hordes of tourists and walkers. Alfie neglected to add that it was only half of these tourists, the girls, in whom he was particularly interested. Nonetheless, Cap could fill in the omitted details and the request was granted, with just, "OK, kid, you got it."

"It's closing time"...

In most states, the state itself dictates bar closing times. Not so in New Jersey. Throughout the years, last call in Wildwood bars came at different times. In 1976, the year of this story, closing time in Wildwood came at two a.m., as dictated by the town itself. Bartenders like to say, "You don't have to go home, but you can't stay here." One bar in town, in order to expedite the exodus, played bagpipe "music" at full blast.

In practical terms, before one-thirty, a bar-goer in the town of Wildwood had to decide which bar they wanted to close, since no was admitted into a bar after that time. This played perfectly into the lifeguards' routine. As bar time was running out, they could offer the ladies the chance to continue the party back at their place, have a few more drinks, have some fun in the bed, and be asleep early enough to get six or seven hours sleep, and feel relatively fresh in the morning.

Surrounding municipalities, in a ploy to attract late revelers, extended their closing time to 5 a.m. Occasionally, guards would fall into the trap, and then have to pray for rain in the morning. As they would awaken to the alarm at eight-thirty, they would peer out their window and harken back to the old maritime adage, "Red sky at night, sailor's delight. Red sky by morning, sailor, take warning."

On those uncomfortably inclement days, when a hungover lifeguard *did* have to man his stand, Clem and Dunes of stand # 9, both being veteran lifeguards who could thoroughly depend on each other, had special methods to alternately catch up on their sleep, nice and dry under their umbrella. As most guards did, they had a "toe board," a 1 x 4 inch plank that they inserted in between the back slats of their stand and it went out five feet or so, giving the guard a comfortable surface on which to extend and rest their legs. Then, the "sleeper" would roll a towel up and tie it around his neck, so that his head wouldn't be "pecking corn." With the towel in place and the hood on the lifeguard jacket up, it gave the appearance that the lifeguard was intently watching the water. The lads also had a pair of those very dark, skiing-style sunglasses that had leather side panels to block out all peripheral light. One more piece of equipment made the outfit complete: they had a pair of cloth gardening gloves, which they had sewn together, so that when the sleeper had his crossed knee up, his hands wouldn't slip apart and lose their grip on the knee. With all these features in place, the boys would just alternate their surreptitious bouts of sleep.

In later years Wildwood went to a five a.m. closing, so as to keep the business of those who might flee to another town to keep drinking after two. The outcome of this was that no one interested in bar life would go out before one in the morning. Consequently, if one were to go out for a drink at a reasonable hour, say ten at night, they might find themselves alone in the bar.

Tuesday, June 22nd
Kissin Time Bobby Rydell

When Harry's rookie, Steve was called off the stand for some water action, Walt the Salt ran down to sit up with Harry on stand # 2. Besides getting Walt closer to the ongoing rescue, it was also time to compare some notes. Over the last few days, Walt had noticed a certain honey spending time down at Harry's stand and asked, "What's your interest in that Suzie? I devoted a whole boring night to that girl. I romanced her, took her back to my pad, where we drank some *Bali Hi* wine together and it seemed that all was going well. At that point, I thought that there would surely be some fun in store, but when it got around to the intimacy part, that girl wouldn't even kiss me. Even so, I remained a gentleman, all the while looking at the door that would get me out to the bars."

So, Walt just had to ask, "Harry, what's the scoop here? Is your interest in this girl strictly platonic, or what?" To which, Harry had quite a laugh. 'Walt, I'll tell you the truth. I had a *really* wild night with Suzie." Now, totally puzzled, Walt had to ask, "How could that be? Did she like you that much more than me?" With a bit of a snicker, Harry related, "No, Walt, she just didn't like to kiss, that's all. She loved to fuck. She just didn't like kissing. She thought it was too personal." *Lesson taken.*

Getting cards and letters from people I don't even know...

"You know, Jeff," Alfie was saying, "this morning I got these three letters from three girls that I can't place. I wish they'd give me a clue or two about when we were together. Maybe, say when they were down at *the Shore.* A photo would really help. But, all that each of them says is, 'What a great time I had, and that I hope to get down again.' Two of the postmarks are from Philly, so that's no help, and the other one is stamped 'Reading, Pa.' I don't remember meeting any honeys form Reading, do you? A couple of weeks ago, I got one of these "anonymous" letters, telling me just how "insincere" I was. I'll have to admit, I guess I do get a little insincere during the summer. I have thought about taking pictures of my hook-ups, but, then, by the time I'd get the film developed, I'd have forgotten who the ladies were anyway, just like now. Oh well, if they do return, I'm sure it'll come back to me and I'll just have you ask them what their names are. OK?" "You got it, Alf."

The Magical Deuce...

In life, most great jobs, of which there are certainly very few, pay comparatively little. Like the old joke, "We get paid weekly, very weakly!" This surely pertained to the Wildwood Beach Patrol job. Most of the veteran guards would say that they would work the job for nothing, and that was absolutely true, because the nearly did. "City hall" knew this and paid accordingly. Beach patrols that were unionized, like the Atlantic City Beach Patrol, did pay well, but most South Jersey beach patrols in the seventies hadn't yet been unionized. By getting paid so little (about $150 a week gross for a forty-eight-hour week) and getting a check bi-weekly, the average partying lifeguard would run out of the cash by the end of the first week.

What to do now? Well, borrow, of course. But, often it was time to go out to the bars and there was no one around to "touch." The solution was to be found in a phenomenon lifeguards referred to as the *magical deuce,* the premise of which was that you needed only two dollars to prime the pump, that is, two dollars was enough back then to buy a few beers in a crowded bar, and that, once there, you'd certainly run into some friend from whom to borrow enough for that night out. On payday Friday, a week or so later, one would find all of the debtors and the creditors at the *First Union Trust Bank* settling their accounts. Not too long afterward, the bi-weekly cycle of loan and debt would begin all over again.

Wednesday, June 23rd

Now, after almost two weeks, of Jeff's being under Alfie's tutelage. Alfie posed a tricky question for Jeff to think over and answer, "As a rookie this summer, what is your most important job" Jeff took little time to respond, "Watching the water," to which, Alfie smiled and said, "No." Jeff took a few more stabs at the answer and gave up. "Most important of all is getting liked," Alfie told him, and, continued with, "Every year a few of the first-year guys from the previous summer don't get asked back, mostly because they weren't liked. They might have been know-it-alls or they may have been boasters or whatever, but at the heart of the matter was that they weren't liked. So, my advice to you, Jeff, is to be a good listener and, in general, be a pleasant guy."

A few weeks later, Alfie followed up on "most important" aspects of the job by asking Jeff, "Besides getting liked, what's the second-most important duty you have in reference to beach mechanics or beach operation?" Again Jeff gave the logical responses, like, "Watching the water, etc." Eventually, Alfie filled him in, "No, it's seeing the jeep before it sees us. The brass gets to see each of the guys on their stands just a few times a day, forming a sort of snapshot of the kind of job they do, so seeing the jeep from a long way off gives each stand the ability to dress up the impression that the bosses get. And, *that's* really important."

Thursday, June 24th
All by Myself Eric Carmen

Not all of the friends of the veteran guards who took the lifeguard test made it. But, there *were* other summer opportunities for lifeguarding, albeit, far down the social ladder from working as an ocean lifeguard. And, each had varying degrees of spotlight

53

for meeting honeys. One friend of a few of the Wildwood lifeguards was a young jitterbug named Raymond. "I really had my heart set on getting the lifeguard job," he had said more than once. But, there came about a silver lining for Raymond. He ended up taking a job on a lake that was within an offshore campground, one that was favored by the many French-Canadians who would drive the eight hours or so down to the Jersey Cape to vacation.

When asked by his pals, some of the Wildwood guards, "How are you making out with the Frenchies?" Raymond enthused about how beautiful lots of the girls were, but the greatest drawback, however, was that they were mostly French-Canadians, who spoke little or no English. Alfie had studied a few semesters of college French over off-season winters, with the motivation of getting the upper hand with the many *jeune filles* who came to the beach with or without their families. To have a bit of fun, Alfie gave Raymond a phrase that would fill in a lot of the blanks, one purported to have a lot of good meanings, something like *Aloha* has in Hawaii or *Prego* in Italy. "Raymond, just say to them. '*A tu pete?*' and give them a big smile."

And, when delivered with Raymond's *aw shucks* grin, it really did get the girls smiling and giggling in return. Not until after half the summer had gone by did Raymond discover that he had been coached to ask, *"A tu pete"* ("Did you fart?" in French). Zany as he was, Raymond knew a good thing when he came across one and he continued to open conversations with, *"A tu pete"* despite knowing how it translated. Who could argue with it if it made the girls smile and laugh? Wasn't that, after all, the first step to getting in there?

Thursday, June 24th
Plans...

Hillary and Stephanie, two hip young New York professionals were able to escape the dreaded weekend drive to Wildwood by taking a Friday personal day and leaving on Thursday after work. "Come on, Hill, we have mounds of time off coming to us. Let's just take off Friday and get a good jump on the weekend at *the Shore*. Then we will have three great days at the beach" Stephanie had said.

In their early twenties, they were beneficiaries of the women's lib/sexual revolution movement. Unconcerned about its political aspects, they enjoyed the social freedoms it allowed. No longer did the specter and ignominy of an unwanted pregnancy hamper the fun. Now, discretion ruled a "good girl's" behavior. What she did with her body was her business, as long as the neighbors and relatives didn't know. And, what better place for anonymity than Wildwood, some one-hundred and thirty miles away from their friends and families in Staten Island. Two and a half hours into the trip and now dusk, from mile marker ten on the Garden State Parkway the huge glimmering Ferris wheel on the Wildwood boardwalk came into view, sending a tacit flush of titillation through each of them. "We're getting close now, Steph. Just smell that beautiful salt sea air." With this light, Thursday south-bound traffic, they'd arrive at land's end for a long weekend of adventure in just about a half an hour. "Let's get to the hotel, shower, and get right out to the bars," Stephanie said, excited at the thought of it. "You bet!" Hillary agreed.

Social Engineering...

Back in the prosperous 50s, with *Shore* properties relatively cheap, the Walsh family, Margaret, John, and the three kids, pressed the budget a bit and bought a nice three-bedroom house on Magnolia Avenue in Wildwood, just a half a block from the beach. Lucky that they were, their three kids got to spend every day of every summer at the beach, where all the "Don'ts" back home resolve into just one at the beach, that is, "Don't throw sand.," making for a carefree atmosphere for both parents and kids. This year, their eldest, John, was on the trimester system at Drexel in Philly and Joan, now twenty, was interning for the summer in a law office. That left just Megan, at eighteen, spending summers at *the Shore* with the family.

For as long as the Walshes could remember, Peter, now a nine-year lifeguard had been stationed on their Magnolia Avenue beach. Through the years he had sort of become one of the family, often being invited over for dinner at the Walsh's. Without being too nosey, Margaret Walsh had observed Peter to be quite gentlemanly with the young ladies who chanced to visit him at his lifeguard stand. For this reason she hatched a rather unconventional plan. On an afternoon when Megan was off on her daily run on the sand, Margaret ambled down to have a chat with Peter. In this permissive age, and despite

Megan's rather strict Catholic upbringing, Mrs. Walsh felt that if her daughter hadn't already lost her virginity, then who better to do it with than Peter. Her plan was to have Peter over for dinner and to very subtly make it known to both Megan and Peter that after dinner she and her husband would be out until late that night, contriving some plausible event that would keep them out of the house. The next morning, without prying or asking a single pointed question, Margaret Walsh inferred from Megan's slightly sheepish demeanor that her social engineering had worked.

As a coed, in a sociology class at Bryn Mawr College, Margaret Walsh had read about this sort of thing happening in Scandinavia, where because of universal conscription into the military for four years, there resulted a severe shortage of eligible bachelors, since before submitting to this sort of *Shanghai,* young men would flee across the border to countries where they'd be free. Consequently, Scandinavian parents with young daughters would invite prospective young men to come stay with the family, even giving the young couple their own room under the parents' roof. Once the daughter got pregnant, the parents had the much-coveted son-in-law.

Friday, June 25th
How Long?   Ace

The prediction delivered unanimously by TV weathermen throughout the Mid-Atlantic States for the coming weekend at the Jersey *Shore* had been, "This weekend will be just beautiful, with air

57

temperatures in the nineties and ocean water temperatures right around 72 degrees." Of course, this would create perfect conditions for clogging all of the major routes to destinations on the South Jersey peninsula.

New York and North-Jersey vacationers would begin their trip in earnest somewhere on the 172-mile Garden State Parkway, the highway whose exits took the number of their mile-marker, prompting the old joke among Jerseyites when meeting outside of the state, "Oh, you're from Jersey? What exit?" Or, they would put a bumper sticker on their car proclaiming their exit number, like, for instance, an *Exit 0* bumper-sticker would be the Cape May beach exit.

Folks from Pennsylvania, Delaware, and Maryland, could choose the very boring Atlantic City Expressway, and speed at 75 miles an hour through miles and miles of nondescript terrain, or take Route 47, the old *Delsea Drive,* so named from its origin, Delaware to final destination, at the sea and at the foot of the ocean in Wildwood by the Sea. Route 47 was by far the most scenic and also the shortest route. On it, the leisurely south-bound driver would initially pass through farmland, sprinkled with long-since abandoned, but still visually pleasing one- or two-room school houses and small congregational churches. The last forty miles of the trip would course through marshlands, occasionally punctuated by salty creeks cutting under the road, most of which were kept company by crabbers, young and old, eager to fill their bushels with those treasured Jersey blue-pointers.

Somewhere around four this Friday afternoon, *Shorebound* traffic had invaded this bucolic Delsea Drive setting. Riot began to foment, as the backup in southbound cars would grow from a few miles away from the ocean to twenty and sometimes thirty miles away, taking until two or three o'clock Saturday morning to ease the jam. The real blast, however, would come on Saturday. Stoked by the rising heat on this inland road, gridlock would set in early in the day, overheating radiators and tempers at the same time. The less-rational behind the wheel would pointlessly begin beeping their horns, as though this would get the traffic moving. Stalled, these overheated vehicle's drivers would incur the wrath of those stuck behind them. "Come on, you asshole, move it over to the shoulder." And, not uncommonly, right here on Route 47 a fistfight would erupt.

I Get Around   The Beach Boys

Somewhat revealing of the type of adventuresome guys that the seasoned guards were, was the curious fact that almost none flew in from their often far-away winter retreats, like Colorado, New Mexico, Texas, Western Pennsylvania, West Virginia, and Florida, just to mention a few. They mostly drove from these places. Wildwood lifeguards would return from wintering in these interesting locales and by their accounts, fellow guards would be wooed into moving out/down there with them after the summer. Over a few beers at the

59

Terminal Bar, Dollar Bill was telling Alfie's rookie Jeff, "Yeah, you wouldn't believe it but there are these great bars in southeast Denver that have free food and half-priced drinks every weekday happy-hour, and not only free food, but it's great stuff like u-peel 'em shrimp, prime rib, and Alaskan king crab legs, and all for free. For a couple of bucks you can have a nice free dinner and a half-dozen drinks. And, on top of all that, there are loads of babes at these after work, happy-hour bars." But as good as winter times were, when spring rolled around, there were always a few songs that when heard would rev these wintering lifeguards up *wherever* they were. Just about any Beach Boys' tune would do it, but especially, their song about getting back to beach life, *Do It Again.*

A couple of Wildwood lifeguards living it up under a blue-sky afternoon in Colorado.

Walt the Salt and Dollar Bill, who had anchored stands # 3 and #6 for several years made their annual drive in from the mountains of Colorado. Like migratory birds they had the seasons

61

wired. They would drive non-stop, except for gas fill-ups, in Walt's old Chevy *Impala*. Walt had a theory that once you got a car rolling just about any car could make the trip, and that trouble usually arose when the car came to rest. In other years Walt and Bill had made the trip in some real jalopies. A few years back, Walt had walked into a used car lot and said to the salesman, "Look, I have three hundred dollars. Do you have a car for that that will make it back to New Jersey?" So, he bought an old 1963 Plymouth *Valiant*, and it did make it back to Wildwood. In the mountains of Colorado the music may have been John Denver or bluegrass, but once Walt turned the Chevy eastward toward his anticipated summer sojourn there would be but one cassette played until he began the trip in reverse that fall. From June until September, every time the wheels of the Chevy spun, the Beach Boys' *Endless Summer* album played, with tunes like *Surfin' Safari, Catch a Wave, Surfer Girl, the Warmth of the Sun, Surfin' U.S.A,* and *Fun, Fun, Fun* the background music to an entire summer of fun.

Better late than never…

Many avenues have taken these seventy or so lifeguards to becoming Wildwood Beach Patrol ocean lifeguards, but none as peculiar as that of Jim Mc Allister's pathway. To hear him tell it, "I was orphaned by two alcoholic parents in Boston. Before being rescued by my three kindly spinster aunts, we went hungry. I mean, most of the time there was literally *no* food for me and my older brother, Earl. And, to this day that's probably the reason that I'm still a skinny guy. My aunts were devout Catholics, attending mass every morning at six. Growing up in this environment certainly influenced my decision, and at just seventeen, I joined the monastery. But, after 11 years of the monastic life, the edict of silence finally got to me, especially after having been a voluble Irish Catholic teenager.

"At first, after all those years of having my every action dictated to me, I was really lost being out there in society on my own. Luckily, I soon found a position teaching high school English on the outskirts of Boston, where I had the good fortune of teaching with a math teacher by the name of Rick Stevenson. In short order, I became part of Rick's crew, guys that skied on weekends at Stowe Mountain in Vermont. On several occasions on the lift chair, Rick acquainted me with the fun to be had in South Jersey as an ocean lifeguard. At first, I didn't think that would be an appropriate next-step away from the monastery, nonetheless, after some cajoling by Rick, that summer I passed the Wildwood Beach Patrol swim test and got the job, and at 37 years old, became the oldest guy sitting the wood.

"In the beginning, it felt weird, sitting up there on the lifeguard stand, seeing so many good-looking young ladies passing by in their bikinis, but after a while, I began to feel comfortable with it. Before joining the monastery, I had had only one girlfriend, so this 'dating' thing was all new to me. And, it rather shocked me that pretty girls could actually be interested in *me*. But now, after three years of lifeguarding, I've come to realize that becoming an ocean lifeguard was my redemption. I shudder to think how things might have turned out for me had I not met Rick and the guys. I might have had to lead a reclusive life, remaining outside of society. Joining the Wildwood Beach Patrol gave me great camaraderie with lots of terrific friends and a smooth path to meeting some really sweet ladies." As time went on, Jim McAllister recaptured more and more of his own identity and the self-confidence that had been denied by monastic life. From the shy, retiring guy who had first joined the beach patrol, friends now considered him "the life of the party."

Friday, June 25th

This year, WBP had hired a kid that had finished the swim test quite a few places off the pack that had qualified for rookie school. Ferris Wooding, now sitting Stand #1 with eight-year veteran, Bobby Morrison, had said something to Lieutenant Shelly a few days before the test was to be given, that is, he said, "All my life I have wanted to become a Wildwood lifeguard." Upon hearing this, Shelly immediately liked the kid's attitude and after the swim test he moved him up into the selected group of rookies chosen for rookie school. With a little coaching on stroke mechanics, the lieutenant thought, Ferris would be right in step with most of the other first-year guys.

Ferris had been a lucky kid. When he was still a toddler his parents had bought a three-bedroom summer bungalow just one block from the beach in Wildwood on Rio Grande Avenue. He had spent virtually every summer day of his life on the beach. Early in his experience on the sand, the daringness of ocean rescues brought his admiration, as he would squeeze his way through the large crowds that would gather to see those oft'times dazed victims being brought out of the water by those heroic lifeguards. Then, as puberty mysteriously took hold of Ferris, it was the cuties stopping by to talk with the lifeguards that caught his attention. Feigning interest in some bit of sea life that had washed up close-by the lifeguard stand, Ferris would eavesdrop on conversations, overhearing the customary lifeguard lines like "What are you ladies doing tonight?" or "Let's get together tonight and have some real fun." And, so the seed of one day becoming a lifeguard was firmly planted.

As his adolescent years went by, Ferris thought a lot about passing that lifeguard test when he got to be old enough. But, as puberty came upon him he felt a bit left behind. His classmates, the boys, were beginning to sprout up at the ages of fourteen and fifteen, yet at fifteen, Ferris was but five-foot-three. In all of his summers on the beach he couldn't recall ever seeing a really short lifeguard. Then, by his sixteenth summer, he had quite fortunately attained the grand height of five feet five, still rather diminutive by lifeguard standards. But, luckily, though, attitude accounted for more to Lieutenant Shelly than polished swimming ability or the kid's height. Because of his small stature while growing up, he had developed a bit if shyness, but as we shall see, Ferris, along with the other rookies, wouldn't recognize that image of himself in the mirror, either, after a few weeks on the lifeguard stand.

Bobby and Ferris, on stand # 1 probably had the toughest stand of the beach patrol to work, and today, a big surf day, would give testament to that. Their stand sat right next to an amusement pier that extended a hundred yards or more into the surf at high tide. It was also the destination beach for busloads of city folk, most of whom were non-swimmers, and some had never, in fact, even seen a beach before. To stay in touch with the lifeguards to the south of them the two lifeguard stands had to be aligned so as to be seen by one another through the pilings of a two-hundred-yard-wide pier. Bobby and Ferris' stand had an amusement ride called the *Himalaya* next to them to the south and above them, a ride that played but one song at full-blast the entire summer, Sam the Sham and the Pharaohs' *Woolly Bully*. Often a guard would have to run halfway through the long pier just to pass the whistle signal over the din above.

On this day out in front of them, three adult bathers were beginning to be swept toward the pilings of the pier by the southward drift. When Bobby called the run, the trio of victims was just twenty yards away from the pilings, which were in six to eight feet of swirling water. By the time the guards coming in from the north side of the pier got to them, they were well into the pilings. Veteran guards knew to discard their rescue buoys before swimming into this maze of pilings under the pier, since the six feet of rope attaching a lifeguard to his rescue buoy would just complicate the rescue by getting tangled around pilings. A few rookies stayed connected to their rescue buoys and became so restricted by their tangled ropes that they became useless to the rescue.

Bobby, Clem, and a few of the lifeguards more experienced with pier rescues, cross-chested the victims, kept them away from the pilings as best they could, and with the help of the south drift progressively bobbed their victims safely to the leeward side of the pier, where a long chain of lifeguards from the south side of the pier towed them in to safety. Both the guards and their victims got a bit scraped up by the barnacles on the pilings, but none were seriously hurt. Remarkably, days on end could pass without a single rescue, but then one like this one brought it home to you why you trained so hard and made you realize the real skill entailed in making such a complicated rescue.

The last weekend in June...
Get Down Tonight
KC and the Sunshine Band

Hillary and Stephanie, the New York girls, had the weekend thoroughly mapped out. The weatherman had been right--the weather was just perfect for the weekend. "Hill, we should be able head for the beach by ten every day and have full days on that fine crystalline sand," Stephanie said, "and then at around three or so we can head back to the hotel to shower up and get sexy for our favorite afternoon social, at the *Southwind Bar*." This was the bar where every ten minutes or so one of the bartenders would spin the wheel and where it would come to rest, that would determine the price of drinks until the next spin. This afternoon a casual atmosphere pervaded the bar, with lots of the enthusiasts still in bathing suits and with the *pina coladas* and the rum-cokes free-flowing. Hillary reminded Stephanie, "Now remember, if one of us meets and wants to go off with some new hunk, neither of us will feel abandoned. But, just let the one of us who stays behind in the *Southwind* know whether you're going to his place or to our hotel room, so that we'll know which place is open should the whim move the second one of us to hook up with a guy."

Reading this today, one might consider this somewhat aberrant behavior, yet one need only look at the July 10th, 1976 *Billboard Top 100* popular music chart and see that the number one song in the USA for that date was, *Afternoon Delight*, by The Starland Vocal Band. How different the social norms were back then, when a "quickie" in the afternoon wouldn't have raised an eyebrow. Later in the evenings, Hillary and Stephanie would bar hop together, walking along Pacific Avenue and cruising the many night spots that got cooking at around ten.

Saturday, June 26th

Besides the *Southwind* and its *Spin-the-Wheel* happy hour, afternoons also got rockin' at the *Barefoot Bar,* with the live music of the hard-drinking, one-man riot named Billy Jack. With just a bit of canned back-beat and a guitar and his sometimes-harmonica, you'd think you were at a

68

four-man-band rock concert. Enthusiasts began drifting in off the beach at around three and by five the place wailed. With the *pina coladas* and rum and cokes in abundance on the bar, the crowd got charged up on Billy Jack's rasp of a voice, belting out lots of Stones' tunes, favorite among which was *Satisfaction.*

Getting the early knockoff this rainy Saturday, Alfie got to the *Barefoot* by four, to find the bar at full speed. With the push of a few rum and cokes he accelerated to the pace of the crowd, and in no time found himself a semi-inebriated brown-eyed cutie named Jackie to keep him company. That she slightly slurred the, "Hi, I'm Jackie from Jersey City," and gave him a sultry wink alerted Alfie that this girl might be up for a little real fun. So, with Buffet offering the suggestion, *Why Don't We Get Drunk and Screw*, the couple soon found themselves on a commode in a stall in the ladies room doing just that. "Are you sure it's alright," she had asked. "Sure, people do it all the time in this crazy bar," Alfie reassured her.

Trying to keep as quiet as possible to avoid drawing attention to themselves, while at the same time enjoying the spontaneity of the moment, they heard a female giggle, accompanied by a male, "Shush," coming from what seemed to be the next stall. Coincidentally, both couples emerged from their hiding places at the same time, and Alfie saw that the stocky blond-haired guy was the one that he had seen for years selling newspapers back beach.

The two had never really met but had seen each other "around," in bars and at beach and house parties.

From that chance, ladies' room introduction Alfie and Johnny, "the Paperboy" became fast friends. For years lifeguards would hear the gravel-voiced call of Johnny the Paperboy booming from behind their lifeguard stands. *"Philadelphia Inquirer, New York Daily News, Cosmopolitan, Newsweek..."* And, although at it for over twenty years, and well into his thirties, Johnny insisted on being addressed as "the Paperboy." "Please don't call me the Paperman," he'd say. A bull of a guy, standing about five foot nine, Johnny carried an old-style, strong linen bag with the words, *Philadelphia Inquirer* in faded blue script. Full, it no doubt reached a hundred pounds or more.

Besides the names of publications that he would shout, his stock also included out-of-town newspapers and a wide selection of glossy magazines. As Johnny would say, "I don't just sell these; my real business is 'service'." And, his "service" came at a significant cost. Therefore, the markup on these print publications typically caused a lot of beachgoers an "*ouch!*" when he announced the price. "The prices go up, they don't go down," he'd explain. Or, pointing to the stores on the boardwalk, some four-hundred or more yards off, "You could maybe get a better price up there." he'd retort. His twenty-five cent newspaper went for a dollar and two-dollar magazines went for five. Remarkably, though, even at these exorbitant prices, Johnny the Paperboy would end his day at the beach with an

70

empty bag. By his own account, "I would start the day dead broke and hungover, and by three or four o'clock in the afternoon I'd have an empty paperbag, a fistful of bills, and I'd head on down to the afternoon jam session at the *Barefoot Bar* and wind it up all over again."

Third Rate Romance
The Amazing Rhythm Aces

After becoming lifeguards most guys significantly up their standards in females. Not Ferris, the rookie on Stand #1 with Bobby. He seemed to have gone in the other direction. If a girl or several of them walked the beach totally disregarded by the rest of the lifeguards, then, no doubt, Ferris would stop her or them and set something up for that night. Whether he found this sort of girl more receptive or that he saw something in them that his fellow lifeguards didn't, he had found his niche. Not too long after the other guards observed this *M.O.* in Ferris did he get his nickname, *"Trashman."* Now, one might think that he'd have been insulted when he found out, but quite the opposite happened. Somehow or other, he loved the celebrity in the name, asking people to call him Trashman, rather than Ferris.

Ferris, who was from Sharon Hill, Pa. had gone in on a place for the summer with five of his buddies from back home. Most of them came down only on weekends, so during the weekdays Ferris had the run of the place to himself. When Fred, one of his roommates in the house *was* there, they shared a big bedroom with two double beds. Before the summer started Ferris thought this a comfortable arrangement, but now that he was a lifeguard and having great success with the ladies, problems arose, namely, he didn't have a private bedroom for his hook-ups. Because Fred, a very mild-mannered guy was usually in bed by ten, Ferris had devised a way to get around this indelicacy. When Ferris would arrive later and lead the prospective young lady to his bedroom, she would invariably say, "Oh, your roommate is asleep. We can't do anything with him here." To which, Ferris would give his stock response, "Oh, Fred, he got really drunk earlier today and passed out, so don't worry about him hearing anything." Surprisingly, this usually worked, although from time to time there *did* come a faint embarrassed whimper out from under Fred's covers.

Sunday, June 27th

Today, the "postcard day" fell apart at around three. An ominous black-purple tube of a cloud began to work its way north, suddenly bringing heavy winds and driving rains to the beach and ocean. The rumble of thunder had preceded this fast-moving cell. Guards who had had their umbrellas up hastily took them down until the lightning passed, for fear of them becoming lightning rods. Bathers who weren't beach-savvy enough to act on their own were called out of the water for fear of lightning striking the ocean. A mass exodus ensued, as folks who just ten minutes beforehand had been enjoying a beautiful sunny day. Beach chairs, blankets, and kids were scooped up as fat drops of rain pelted the retreating crowds. Like other smart lifeguards up and down the beach, Alfie and Jeff took refuge under their wooden lifeguard stand, knowing that just as quickly as the rain had begun it would probably be over in a short while. Then, as if as on cue, the clouds did move out, continuing their northern run, sunshine was restored. Over the next few hours leading up to knock-off, a few stragglers began to make their way to the sand, and some back into the ocean. Most folks who had left, though, were content with the day at the beach that they had had, and stayed back at their hotels.

Alfie and Jeff climbed back up on the stand and resumed their scan of the water. With just a handful of bathers to watch. Jeff thought this an apt opportunity to ask Alfie just how he got started in lifeguarding. Alfie though the question over for a little while before sailing in with his reply. "Well, Jeff, I'd been coming to Wildwood beach for as long as I can remember, first as a kid with my parents and then all through high school summers. The summer in betwcen my sophomore and junior years of high school, my folks let me work at *the Shore*. I had a neighborhood buddy who had a free summer place to stay in Wildwood. It was a first floor apartment with almost no ventilation. We slept on two single beds, my pal Winston's bed was right next to a big picture window adjacent to the sidewalk on the other side of the glass. Too hot to wear anything to sleep, we slept in the nude. A few times, before leaving for my five a.m. starting-time at the boardwalk bicycle rentals job, I would draw the curtain back all the way, leaving Winnie on display in the buff for a few hours

73

until he woke up. He would come down to the bike rental shop just fuming, but after a while, even he saw the great humor in it.

"In the last couple of years of high school and the first few of college, my pals and I from the neighborhood used to 'thumb' down *the Shore*, much over our parents objections and generous offers to pay the bus fare. We just found a lot of adventure in hitchhiking. Back then people weren't so paranoid, and would give you a ride just to have a little conversation. The few times that we had taken the bus, we'd been bored stiff, especially when the bus that you arrived to take from the downtown Philly Transit of New Jersey bus terminal was a 'local,' making many, many stops, turning the normal two-hour trip into well over three.

"Back when I was in high school," Alfie continued, "there was this nebbish of a guy named Jack Hammond, who, during the school year would have had trouble getting a date, but who in the summer had girls falling all over him because he lifeguarded on the beach in Wildwood. He would go from a prince in the summer and to a pawn in the winter.

"My swimming background was that I had learned to swim by intuition, that is, without the benefit of any formal instruction, in a city pool with hundreds of kids in the water and lots of maniacs cannon-balling all around. I didn't get around to trying out for the guards until I was three years out of high school. I knew the younger brother of one of the older guards named Al, and he arranged to get me an

individual test, in which they told me to swim out
behind the lifeboat that my pal's older brud was
rowing. At that stage in my swimming development,
I was still unable to swim with my face in the water.
It seemed to me that Al was rowing to France. After
about what was in reality only about two hundred
yards, they pulled me into the boat. Test concluded,
'Come back next summer and try again.'

Y.M.C.A. **Village People**

"That dreadful experience sent me to the
neighborhood YMCA pool the next winter. A couple
of my other buddies who aspired to the beach patrol
went with me for the preliminary physical. The first
of them came out after his physical exam and told us,
'Wow, wait 'til you see the nurse. She's a really sexy
young brunette with really nice boobs.' The ruse
surely worked on me. When I went in to see the
'nurse' I had this killer erection and a beet-red face
on entering the room to be examined by the wizened
old male doctor.

"At the 'Y,' my pals and I swam the one-hour
sessions a couple of times a week for the four
months leading up to the June beach test. That day in
'66 they took the first thirteen guys out of the water;
however, I had come in fourteenth and was made an
'alternate.' None of my other cohorts made it.
Unfortunately, they didn't know the Jack Hammond
story about becoming a chick magnet on the stand as
a Wildwood Beach Patrol lifeguard. I kept going
back and back to the Wildwood B.P. headquarters to
see if there had been an opening. As it turned out,
one of the veteran guards that they were holding a

spot open for didn't return, and through persistence, I did finally--two weeks later--get on with the guards, during which time the other thirteen rookies had been trained in the two weeks of 'rookie school.'

"They gave me a 'can'" (a lifeguard flotation buoy), an *Acme Thunderer* whistle on a lanyard, a pair of white linen shorts, and a red tank top with the letters WBP splashed across the chest. I knew what to do with the shorts and redtop, but hadn't the faintest idea of what to do with either the whistle or the can. That first summer on the wood there must have been a half-dozen or more rescues called in my water by guards sitting at stands next to me. I had such a miserable performance year that upon returning the next summer I had been placed on the 'Do not rehire' list. And, it was only after pleading with Captain Capacio that I *was* rehired as 'on probation.' A very shaky start to what is now 11 years on the wood."

Monday, June 28th
"And going with it as it went,
all I knew of discontent."
The Abdication of King Fergus

Out on boat patrol, Alfie was telling one of the rookies, "You know, kid, when I started 'working the beach' 11 years ago there was an old-timer named Aubs who had been sitting the wood for upwards of 20 years. During that time he had staunchly resisted the temptation of 'moving up,' that is, becoming part of the management team, the jeep drivers and lieutenants. Aubs contended that to do so would move you farther and farther away from the water's edge, and that that's was where the real lifeguarding went on and where the real fun of the job happened.

"A few years later, I got to know all too well just what Aubs was talking about. When I had come back for my seventh summer of lifeguarding, Captain Capacio wanted to make me a lieutenant, meaning that I would be in charge of the thirteen lifeguard stands, on which all of my friends worked. With a great deal of reluctance, I did take the 'promotion.' Almost immediately, I detected a change in my relationship with the lifeguards. I was no longer one of the boys. I became someone to be regarded with suspicion. To please Cap, though, I did keep at it for over a month, but, the last straw was that Cap had called me into his office one day and said, 'Now, Alfie, since you're a lieutenant, you have to behave better than the rest of the guys on the patrol. The late hours and the drinking have to be toned way down.' I thought to myself, 'I didn't learn to swim to be in charge of people, and especially not to be in charge of my good friends. This lieutenant job has taken the fun out of working the beach.' And, with that, I humbly resigned the 'promotion' and went back to 'sitting the wood.' Aubs was totally right. The *wood* is where it's at, or, simply, "The wood is good!"

"On a few occasions during which my and Aubs' time on the beach coincided, we had briefly spent a few days together 'sitting up.' There resided a lot of beach wisdom in Aubs, accumulated over all those years. One notion that I picked up from Aubs was when he said, 'No matter how long you've been working the beach, today you're going to see something you've never seen before. All you need to do is really pay attention.' To me, this seemed at first to be something of an exaggeration, but, eventually, I came to believe it to be absolutely true. From seeing a woman on the beach reading a paperback while walking backwards to witnessing 'Hank the Waiter' emerge from the breakers, fully-outfitted in his waiter uniform, balancing a tray with two martini glasses on it, every day at the beach does hold something original.

"Another of Aubs' tenants, as he put it was, 'As you spent more and more years on the wood, your scanning of the water becomes more and more second-natured, which serves a working lifeguard well. The seasoned lifeguard would be scanning without really thinking about it. In fact, there were, no doubt, times when on the beach an old fussbudget would get a shock when the whistles went off, signaling a rescue, since she was absolutely certain that 'this guard wasn't paying any attention to the bathers.' The drawback to 'scanning' came in the away-from-the-stand time, when someone that the off-duty lifeguard happened to be talking to felt that he wasn't paying attention to them, or, worse, when a prospective female sensed that the off-duty guard was looking around for 'something better.'"

Tuesday, June 29th
In the Warmth of the Sun
The Beach Boys

Along with the official hand signals that were sent up and down the beach (like the water rescue and the land emergency signals) the Wildwood lifeguards had other unofficial but well-recognized signals. A lifeguard spinning his fists around one another was the signal for a "runner," that is, someone to go back to the boardwalk for eats or drinks. Today, Seadog whistled down to Peter O'Neill, held up his radio, while pointing to it with his other hand. This was the signal that there was a song playing that they liked, in this case it was the Beach Boys, singing *Rock and Roll Music.*

The term, *beach boys*, no doubt had its origin from the local Hawai'ian guys that gave surfing lessons and outrigger canoe rides from the beach in Waikiki. "America's band," the *Beach Boys,* were, in a way, martyrs to the beach-life cause, in that, as legend went, they rarely partook of the joys to be had at and around the beach. They created this wonderfully inspiring beach-associated music, while others lived it. To South Jersey lifeguards the words to so many of their songs were anthem. Ocean lifeguards felt that the tunes were almost written especially for them. *The Girls on the Beach, Catch a Wave, Do It Again, Surfin' U.S.A.,* to name just a few.

Wednesday June 30th
When I Grow Up to Be a Man
  The Beach Boys

     On stand # 4 Harry and his rookie, Steve were enjoying this fine summer day, sitting back and listening to the Beach Boys singing *When I Grow Up (To Be a Man),* when Harry recalled something that he remembered happening 10 years ago, in his rookie year, when he was just eighteen. "I was sitting with a thirty-year-old guard named Jack Dooley, and, I thought it a bit odd when the senior lifeguard from the next stand, a guy in his late twenties, took a walk down to our stand, holding in his hand a transistor radio, and, on it was playing the *Beach Boys'* newest tune, *Darlin'.* 'You gotta hear this, Jack. It's their latest. I've heard it only twice and I love it already.' At the time, I just didn't get it, how these two 'old guys' could still be interested in this 'young-style' music. But, now *I'm* an 'old guy,' still digging the Beach Boys. Working the beach is really a special place where you don't have to grow up." And, Wildwood Beach Patrol in the seventies made protracted adolescence both highly desirable and respectable. After all, these boys *were* saving lives.

Since Alfie had been on the job and around the beach for so long, his fellow guards had come to trust his ability to forecast the weather. Often, as clouds moved in, the jeep crew would stop by his stand and ask, "Rain?" Pushing his reputation a little, he might respond, "Yeah, at around three" or "No, with that patch of blue sky off to the west, this'll move out after a brief sprinkle." All things considered, Alfie's knowledge of weather was quite solid.

On one point concerning weather, he scored 100 %. And, that was his answer to the question often asked by junior guards. Before heading out to the beach to work they would often ask, "Is today an umbrella day?" In other words, "Should I bring an umbrella to the lifeguard stand today?" At headquarters, every stand had its own designated umbrella, but most guards, especially the ones who had a long, initial walk out to and then back at the end of the day from their stands, were reluctant to bring that cumbersome piece of equipment, the umbrella, along. The standing prediction that Alfie made with complete accuracy to the umbrella question was, "Every day is an umbrella day.

"Even the sunniest morning still has the potential of degenerating into a thunderstorm that afternoon." Sage guards, who invariably made an umbrella part of their standard equipment, got quite a kick out of glancing down beach at two unfortunates standing, huddled under the scant protection from the rain that the wooden planks of their stand's seat provided. As Alfie was fond of saying, "Sometimes you have to pay for the lessons. And, they're often very expensive. There's a lot to be learned when you're out in a rainstorm without an umbrella."

Book 3: July
Thursday, July 1st

Wildwood is a beach where the tide change is about 50 yards from low to the high tide mark, creating a nice flat, hard sand surface. Perfect for strolling. On a strong, "postcard" weather day, and especially so on summer weekends, lifeguards would, no doubt, see thousands of people walk by. The lifeguard stand, from its lofty perch, is what James Thurber, the author, would have called the "catbird seat."

On this fine sunny afternoon a particularly smashing young lady made herself conspicuous by strolling by stand #7 three or four times, paying more than obvious attention to Alfie's rookie, Jeff. With a nudge, Alfie said, "Come on kid, get on that. Call her over." "Oh, Alf, I don't know," in so many words, Jeff shyly intimated that the honey was much too sharp to be interested in him. Alfie knew better. Reluctantly, Jeff did gesture for the hottie to come over, and was relieved when she led the conversation with, "What is there to do here at night." Jeff made a remarkable transition, and even surprised *himself* when he came out with, "Well, I could show you around tonight, if you like." In an instant, she demurred, "Are you sure you don't mind?" "How about I pick you up at seven" And, oh, by the way, my name is Jeff. What's yours?" "Oh, I'm Alice." Little did Jeff realize just how much his attractiveness to the ladies had changed when he had passed the Wildwood Beach Patrol swim test.

83

Obviously, it would take a little time before Jeff took full ownership of his newly-acquired license with the honeys. There were lots of lessons to be learned in the course of this long summer. Surprisingly, once a guy climbs the rungs of the lifeguard stand, his looks don't really matter *all* that much. They do help establish a bit of a pecking order among the lifeguards, but craft and cleverness can often win out over looks, the kind of cleverness that comes with time on the stand.

Summer ocean lifeguards routinely get dates with girls that wouldn't give them a second look in the off-season. Often a guard will stop by the beach on his day off and say hello to lifeguard friends. If he's looking for a honey to spend the day and/or night with, he'll ask the working lifeguard, "Hey, let me borrow your uniform shirt to wear (the shirt with the *WBP* conspicuously emblazoned on the front) so that I can get something going with a honey." With the latitude of being able to walk all around the stand, the day-off lifeguard might say to a passing honey, "Hi, I'm on break now. Would you like to take a walk back to my place and get something cold to drink?" Without that lifeguard shirt, he's just another tourist, but with it on, magic.

Leaving on a Jet Plane
John Denver

One lifeguard exception to the diving mode of returning to work the beach was Seadog, Gary Lieber of stand #11, who spent his winters in Maui, Hawai'i and worked as a water safety instructor and lifeguard at the extravagantly expensive beachfront *Grand Kohio Resort*. When he would leave the Hawai'ian islands for the summer, friends would think he was crazy, "You mean you're really leaving Hawai'i for, of all places, New Joysey?" they'd ask. But Seadog knew better. Not only was he going back to be the cock-of-the-walk (one of many) but he was going back to really superior beaches.

The great advantage of the East Coast beaches is that they are formed by a progression of sand bars and gullies, gradually sounding out to about 26 feet at their deepest, whereas, the much-vaunted, picturesque Hawai'ian beaches and ocean are mostly rocky coastlines of jagged lava and coral. In Hawai'i, very often you have to search for a sandy channel out through the sharp rocks to get out into the ocean. Evidence of this would be where the famed "Pink Hotel," the *Royal Hawai'ian* on Waikiki was built. Directly in front of the hotel lies one of the very few sandy channels on the whole beachfront of Waikiki leading out to deeper water. On most beaches around Hawai'i bodysurfing and simply enjoying the ocean can be a very wary business.

Friday, July 2nd

Not all of the rookies were as hip as young Charley Booth, who, in his rookie year last summer, had been out at the bars just about every night with the veteran guards. Phil, the young rookie rover with Todd needed a little coaxing. On one payday-Friday, all the lifeguards were going to get together at the *Terminal Bar.* The boys had given Phil the big build-up on how good the place was for hooking-up with the ladies. And, in this vein, some of the lads advised him to be sure to bring "protection." Awkwardly, Phil did enter the bar. After a beer or two, a group of jesters asked, "Well, Phil, did you bring protection?" Sheepishly, Phil nodded "yes" and produced a plastic tube of Coppertone SPF 50. This kid had a lot to learn.

A hundred or more beers lined the bar, it being "seven-for-a-dollar" tonight at the *Terminal,* a throwback to former days at an old shot and beer joint, called *McGuire's Four-Leaf Clover Bar.* Clem noticed Phil hanging back from the crowd of guards, nursing a beer. "Hey, Phil, give me twenty, will ya?" he said. Too intimidated to say, "No," Phil dug into his jeans and sorted out a twenty and gave it to Clem. Wondering when he'd get the loan back, his answer came back quickly enough when he got his change of fifteen dollars out of the twenty. "Thanks, Phil, you just bought the boys thirty-five beers." But, as lifeguards always say, "You're only a rookie once."

The Moonshiner
The Clancy Brothers and Tommy Makem

Having grown up in the inter city, Clem certainly had a hard edge to him. The rough and tumble of the neighborhood had put its stamp on him. Back then, Clem was what people would call "a real piece of work." On one of their rides north for another summer, Ryan had remarked to Clem, "You know what I like most about you is that you don't give a hoot about what people think." And, despite friendly kidding from his buddies about his sometimes crude behavior, Clem just sailed on unaffected by the criticism. He had the attitude like in the words of the old Irish ballad, *The Moonshiner,* "Well, if you don't like me then leave me alone." And, surely, lots of people did just that, but, lots of others *did* like him and were friends. Probably, his most appealing quality was that there was no pretentiousness about him. Totally brash, but, at the same time totally sincere. He was certainly a plain dealer.

What, you're going to
New Joisey for the summer?

What most Americans don't realize about the much-maligned state of New Jersey is that as one moves southward toward the Jersey Cape, roughly in the middle of the state there are to be found what are called the rather pristine "pine barrens," encompassing about fifty miles of land north to south and spanning from the longitudinal center of the state on the west to the Atlantic Ocean eastward, before one gets into the expansive *Shore* region of marshland, back bays, and ocean front beaches. The *Pinelands,* as it is often called, is a densely forested coastal plain, encompassing seven New Jersey counties. Early settlers found the soil totally unsuitable for farming, hence the term "pine barrens." Most of New Jersey's bad reputation derives from the areas directly in contact with New York, across the Hudson River, areas that have been heavily commercialized, and, hence, "trashed." In truth, the greater majority of New Jersey counties are quite beautiful, and, this is especially so of the Jersey *Shore.*

Another consideration in favor of the Jersey *Shore* was that when Alfie took the lifeguard swim test in 1966, a swimmer couldn't see his extended hand in front of him, due to the fact that they were dumping treated sewage one mile off shore. *Imagine!* A few years later it went to 12 miles, and then 112 miles, until the dumping was finally eliminated altogether. Consequently, it has evolved that the ocean water in South Jersey has become so clear that today one can often see the sand ripples on the ocean bottom while in chest-deep water.

Summer in the City
  The Lovin' Spoonful

As anyone who has spent summers on the
East Coast knows, the big cities go through heat-
waves, with all that concrete often holding the
mercury near or above the 100-degree mark. Seeking
relief, droves of city dwellers mass to beach resort
towns on weekends. The TV weatherman, with
predictions of steamy weekend weather, has a lot to
do with these migrations. Met with these sweltering
city temperatures, people talk all weeklong about
"getting down to *the Shore." Ah, the beach!*
Typically, once there, the onshore sea breeze
develops at round two o'clock, bringing nature's air
conditioning to the beach chairs and blankets. Until
then there is always the cool, beckoning ocean, with
its temperatures soothingly in the seventies. Atlantic
City, once "the Nation's Playground," started this
trend of summer escape back in the 1890s and it has
flourished ever since.

Alfie recalled to Jeff one extraordinary day at
the beach in July a few years ago. On that day, as the
mainland, that is, any land mass west of the barrier
islands that form the Jersey *Shore,* roasted, a brisk
off-shore wind developed and was at work cleaving
off the upper layers of warm ocean water, bring an
upwelling of very cold water to the surface. From the
radio on their lifeguard stands, Wildwood lifeguards
heard DJs report, "Currently, ocean temperatures in
South Jersey have dipped to fifty-five degrees. On
the beaches of South Jersey, air temperature is at

89

seventy-seven degrees, and, inland the mercury sits at ninety-nine degrees. "Imagine that, Jeff, a forty-degree difference between the ocean and the mainland, and the two are only about a mile or two apart." Remembering that day, Alfie added, "Yeah, and it wasn't long before that frigid ocean water chilled the humid air just above it and a thick fog set in over the ocean, and stayed until the wind shifted to onshore later that afternoon. Everyone who worked that day will especially remember it since with visibility at nearly zero, the lifeguards had to go out in that bone-chilling water on "can patrol" to make sure that no bathers slipped beyond where they could be seen and protected.

Saturday, July 3rd
It Only Takes a Minute (to fall in love)
   Tavares
      On weekdays, Alfie typically does a runs-swim-run workout after the 5:30 knock-off, but today, Friday, he's in a sweat to get to the *Spin-the-Wheel* at the *Southwind*, since it will, no doubt, be packed with semi-inebriated beach bunnies. On his way to his locker on the second floor of beach headquarters, he asked a few of the guards that happened to be within earshot, "You guys going over to the *Southwind?*" Alfie laughed when a few of them said, "Naw, we got to go home to shower and change, and it'll be over by the time I get there." "You boys *do* know that we have a shower here at HQ, don't you? Why don't you lads keep fresh clothes in your locker, then, you'd only have to go home if you had a girl or if you wanted to go home

90

to sleep?" Alfie thought to himself, "Some guys don't catch on to just how short a summer is." After a quick shower, Alfie changed into clothes from his locker "wardrobe." He took a quick look in the mirror, combed his flaxen hair, and thought to himself, *I'd do me if I were girl.*

A dozen or so of Alfie's fellow lifeguards had rushed over to the *Southwind*, as well, all waiting to stock up on drinks when the wheel would stop on a low drink price, ideally at the bottom price of nineteen cents a drink. Hillary and Stephanie, the New York dollies, certainly stood out, in that their level of sophistication and stylish sundresses put them in a class of their own when seen against the rest of the females there. Both had sharply-cut V-lines to their sun dresses, nicely exposing their voluptuous bosoms, made even sexier by their semi-exposed tan lines. Having a bit of a fetish for redheads, Alfie locked on to Stephanie's green eyes in an instant. The notion of "the fire down below" gave him a stir. Their eyes met and chemistry took over.

On their short drive from the *Southwind* to Stephanie's hotel, the *Zephyr*, Alfie had to keep his excitement guarded. He knew that he had something special here. The girls had brought down some fine New York white zinfandel, and over a chilled glass of the wine, Alfie sensed from Stephanie's alluring smile that they'd be in bed together before too long. Alfie apprehended her on her way back from locking the hotel room door, and they kissed like long-lost lovers. At the *Southwind Bar*, he had seen most of

91

those gorgeous titties, but now as her string-top bra fell away, the beauty was complete. As they kissed and enjoyed exploring each other's body, Alfie's hand came to rest on her magnificent ass, with just a small area covered by her pink thong. With the untying of a single bow, that, too, fell to the carpet. As they took it to the bed, Alfie glanced down and saw fine wisps of her strawberry blonde pubes, which had been seductively shaved into a heart, the point of which irresistibly drew attention to her glistening pink clit.

At eight o'clock, Alfie reluctantly said good night to Stephanie. She had told Alfie on their ride to the *Zephyr* that, "No matter what, Hillary and I have agreed to give each other company for our nightly barhop." Without a word spoken between the lovers, they tacitly knew that they would be at the *Southwind* tomorrow for another juicy rendezvous.

Sunday, July 4th
Did You Ever Have to Make Up Your Mind?
The Lovin' Spoonful

Down at stand # 5 where Tommy & George held court, the latter was getting the "ultimatum." Over the winter, Jane had become his "main squeeze," and since summer began, she had been coming down for weekends, getting away from her job in "the City," Philadelphia, or as guards like to call Philadelphia, "the shitty." It took just a few visits to the beach for her to pick up on the operation at stand # 5. Returning for just his second year on the wood, George hadn't had much experience with the ultimatum, so he made the unkeepable summer promise, that he would behave himself when Jane was up in the city.

Returning to lifeguarding on the beach for the summer had a way of making the winter girlfriend suddenly seem very ordinary. Typically, these girlfriends have "real jobs" up in the city (whichever city it might be) and would appear in town on odd weekends. Once they got a glimpse of the operation, they often felt compelled to lay down "the ultimatum," which goes something like this, "It's me or the beach this summer" Lifeguards, and especially the veteran guards who knew what an upcoming summer at the beach held, routinely had an easy time handling "the ultimatum." And, more often than not, that was the end of the previous winter's winter romance. . After all, wouldn't it be hard to pick out one shirt off the rack when the salesman says that you can have them all?

Not uncommonly, with exasperation, the "winter girlfriend" would be heard to say, "If I walk away right now, you'll just stop the next pretty girl that passes by." What could a lifeguard say to that? She was absolutely right. That's *exactly* what would happen

The guards who spent their winters in far-off places like Colorado or Hawaii, for instance, were somewhat protected against "the ultimatum," since if they did have a winter girlfriend she would probably either have a summer job or a real job, and would, at best, be only able to come to *the Shore* for a short visit, a week or so. And, although a bit of an interruption in the guard's summer social life, most often he would endure it to have a winter girlfriend when he returned after the summer was over.

In sharp contrast, George's stand partner, Tommy had a different arrangement with his girlfriend of three years, Alison. She had been through the summer transformation in her boyfriend a few times already, and, so had a different approach to the situation. Her summer edict was, "You can screw around when I'm away, but always use a condom. I don't want to catch a disease, and, never ever do the same girl twice. I don't want you falling in love with some bimbo from the beach.

Monday, July 5th
The Girls on the Beach
  The Beach Boys
    On this glistening summer's day at the beach a conspicuous number of young girls strolled the beach with long beach towels wrapped around their waists. "Jeff," Alfie remarked, "Look at those four teenage girls at the water's edge, all with their beach towels wrapped around them, hiding the cottage cheese on their thighs." Lifeguards call the towels the "curtains," the wraps hiding the cellulite. Now, you might think that obesity is a very recent epidemic, but a summer spent observing the passing scene back in the 60s and 70s would tell you that it was a pervasive problem even then. "It's a real shame, but a fact," Alfie continued, "that most honeys roughly over the age of sixteen would typically walk the beach with a full size beach towel wrapped around themselves to conceal the cellulite. Making the problem worse is that for nine months or so a year these east-coast ladies are able to mask the unwanted adipose, aka, fat, with fine clothes. Yeah," Alfie added, "if you were to meet a good looking girl in January, you might not want to be seen with her on the beach in July."
    Not all females suffered this fate. Some held their shape quite well. The general consensus among seasoned guards, those with more than a few years' experience on the wood, was that for pure physical perfection their pick of the litter fell to gymnasts, ice

skaters, or ballerinas. Even as they passed through and then out of teenage, they inexplicably held their shape. On the other hand, as to promiscuity, the magical introductory words that a lifeguard wanted to hear were, "Hi, I'm _____, I'm a nurse." And, even better would be, "I'm a nurse from Pittsburgh.

Ocean lifeguarding, historically.

In 1848 the United States Congress enacted the Newell Act, establishing unmanned lifesaving stations along the New Jersey coast south of New York harbor and to provide "surfboats, rockets, cannonades, and other necessary apparatus for the better preservation of life and property from shipwrecks..." Back then and well into the next century very few Americans knew how to swim well enough to save their own lives, much less being able to rescue others by swimming to their aid. Consequently, as seaside resorts began to become established, corps of lifeguards were organized to protect their ocean-bathing tourists. The Atlantic City Beach Patrol became the very first beach patrol in America in 1891. And, to this day lifeboats are still an integral part of lifeguarding strategy on most of the northeast coast, and especially so on the beaches of South New Jersey.

Tuesday, July 6th
Long May You Run   Neil Young
Morning workouts…

Every other day, stand partners would either set up their lifeguard stand at nine-thirty or they would have the workout. Workouts went on in high seas or calm, rain or shine. In foul weather the whole beach patrol would get to "frolic," that is, *en masse* the boys would hit the heavy surf and just have fun fighting the wild ocean, often current-swept and coming out of the water a mile or more down beach from where they had entered. Early in the season, Captain Capacio would make the workouts runs, usually a three mile round-trip to the fishing pier. Then, as the water warmed up into the seventies,

97

swims were added. By July, the run and swim were combined, and now a real pecking order evolved, since after each morning workout the order of finish, from first to last, was posted in the locker room. And, in the daily list, bragging and teasing rights were founded. Woe betide the goat who shamefully came in last. He'd certainly hear about from the other lifeguards.

Today, Alfie and Bobby, who for years had had their workout rivalry, were in the swim-run event. Bobby the better swimmer, Alfie, had the edge in the run. In the locker room before today's workout Bobby had said, "I don't know, Alf, if I'm getting faster or you're getting slower, but I'm getting pretty close to beating you in this workout." Alfie just smiled, thinking, *Yeah, sure. Talk's cheap.* So, today, after the half-mile in the ocean, predictably, Bobby held a two-minute lead, not usually enough to hold Alfie off in the run, though. True to form, Alfie had Bobby in his sights with 500 meters to the finish. Passing Bobby with just 100 meters to go, Bobby said, "Go get 'em, Alf." With this in his ear, Alfie slowed slightly, knowing he had won it today. But, Bobby had other plans. With only ten meters to go, Bobby accelerated past Alfie, giving him no time to react. Today the race went to the fox.

Jealousy...

Although a close-knit group, from time to time a guy would pass the lifeguard test, work as a guard for a few years, but never really fit in, a guy who shied away from hanging out with the boys at night, preferring to "do his own thing." During his three years on the WBP patrol, Eddie Falbo fit this mold. This sort of individualism doesn't go unnoticed, however, and especially by whomever his stand partner might be, this, primarily because beach bunnies often come in pairs. Without Eddie's cooperation in teaming up with his stand partner, very often the latter missed out on opportunities.

Today, Eddie, now five years removed from working the patrol, had his wife and two little girls at a blanket on the beach behind Alfie's stand. Since he had known Alfie from years ago, he stepped up to the stand and said "Hello," and asked, "What lifeguards are still working the beach from the time I worked?" All the while he furtively ogled the two cuties that Alfie and Jeff had been chatting up. No doubt due to "this geek's" presence, some of the steam went out of the prior conversation, and the girls, who were staying at a hotel on that street, told Alfie and Jeff, "We're going back for lunch but we'll be back after that." Spotting the opening, Eddie said, "Hey, I have to go back to the snack shop at the same hotel that you're staying at and, if you don't mind, I'll walk back with you." Somewhat reluctantly, the ladies did make the trip off the beach with "this Eddie guy." On their way off the beach, Eddie told the girls, "I guess you know that those two lifeguards that you were just talking to are married, and that the older one, 'that Alfie guy,' has a three-year old daughter?" None of this was true, of course. Nonetheless, after that, Alfie and Jeff never saw the girls at any closer range than fifty yards. The lads had become invisible. Deducing what had happened with these two now-reluctant beach honeys, Alfie related to Jeff what his old Irish grandmother had always said about jealousy, "She used to say, 'Jealousy was the only emotion that one couldn't keep inside. When one was jealous, they simply had to do or say something about it. A person could remain mad at someone indefinitely without that person ever knowing about it, but jealousy was another story. It just *had to* come out.'"

Thursday, July 8th
The Hustle   **Van McCoy**

On stand #4 Harry was giving his rook, Steve, some rather unorthodox instruction in the value and use of the surfboat stationed alongside their lifeguard stand. Harry began, "Now, recall, that the Wildwood tide continually moves in and out, with roughly six hours taken in each direction. And, as you know, our lifeguard stand and our surfboat have to be moved continually to maintain a close watch on our bathers. And, this creates a wide expanse of hard sand for strollers. This is especially true at low tide, when female prospects often walk way behind our stand and we lose opportunities to say hello." To wit, Harry coached Steve with, "Whenever we move the stand either to or away from the water, the bow, that's the front, of our twenty-two-foot surfboat has to be placed just off the back of the stand and facing the ocean. The combination of stand and boat creates a thirty-foot barrier, causing the walkers to invariably pass in front us, where we'll have a better chance of introducing ourselves."

The stratagem, which Harry called "the funnel," worked especially well from mid- to high tide. "And, even given this tactical advantage," Harry added, "You must say 'Hello' before a girl passes the 45-degree angle off the front of the stand. Otherwise, she won't have had time enough to react and will feel awkward by being 'put on the spot.' Worse yet, once she's passing directly in front of us she'll have to turn her head back in our direction to respond, which is asking too much of her. We want to make it easy for them to meet us, not hard." Harry further augmented his advice to Steve with, "If an especially good-looking honey that you're interested in gets past you, you're probably not going to see her again, or if you do, she'll be walking fifty yards behind your stand, on the advice of our competition, that is, our fellow lifeguards. And, remember, the ladies are shopping, too. And, even if they commit to seeing you that night, it's not certain unless they come back later in the day to see you. If they *do* return, then you're probably *in.* If they walk way behind your stand, forget them." Harry really had it "wired." The competition referred to stand # 4 as "the Net." Very little of interest got through "the Net."

Friday, July 9th
Band on the Run
   Paul McCartney & Wings
      Rob and Brian on stand # 8, who are really Jack, 25 and Dan, 27, used fake names so as to not get what's called *ratted out.* Age is really an important factor in the evening successes of a

Wildwood lifeguard. Lots of the honeys walking the beach are on vacation with a man, their husband, their boyfriend, or their father, since the cost of some of the nicer hotels and motels in Wildwood by the Sea can a bit pricey. Because the first two categories of females, those with either the boyfriend of husband, are rather unavailable (but, not always) it's the young daughters that are available, and, looking for that dreamed-of date with a bronzed summer lifeguard.

"These younger guys really have it made," Dan was saying to his partner, Jack. "Most of these guys don't have a rap, and if they ever do get laid, it's probably the girl's idea in the first place." In truth, lifeguards from ages from 16 to 19 *are* at the best age for the honeys on the beach. Jack agreed, adding, "Yeah, most of the girls walking the beach have dated guys back home who are either in their class or a year or two older than they are. Guys in their twenties, like us, are 'old guys' to them. That's not to say that they won't be interested in us, but they're usually a little wary since it's a new thing to them, going out with an 'older guy.'" So this is why guards in their twenties lie about their age. "As you know, Dan, "in the daily competition for best-looking girls," Jack added, "the younger guards will use age against us. They'll ask the girls, 'What lifeguards have you ladies met on the beach today?' Then, when they answer, 'Oh, we talked to Rob and Brian,' the younger guards won't know who that was, so, as Rob and Brian we will have avoided 'the rat out.'" So as to avoid the tattlers discovering the ruse, Rob and Brian will become Frank and Stan next week, and on and on. Jack and Dan call the younger guys "the birth certificates," since their age serves as their main, and sometimes only, point of attractiveness with the younger honeys.

"Yeah, and another thing," Dan added, "I really don't like having those young dudes around when we meet girls out at the bars or at a party. We become the "teaser," you know, like in thoroughbred racing. The teaser is the low-quality horse that they put in the stall with the mare that they want to get serviced by the stud, the champion stallion, like the great Secretariat. The teaser gets in there and fusses around with the mare and gets her ready to accept that big dong, and then, just when he's ready to poke her they pull him out and put in Secretariat. They didn't want to take the chance of Secretariat getting injured during the foreplay. And, it's just like that with us and these kids. We have the rap, get the girls laughing and having a good time, and then when it's time to go they leave with the "birth certificates."

Saturday, July 10th

The month of July heralded in one of the highlights of the South Jersey lifeguarding season, the lifeguard races. The thirteen beach patrols from Brigantine, up north, down to Cape May BP formed the South Jersey Lifeguard Association. There were four big races, staged on either a Friday or a Saturday night. Toward the middle of July Wildwood BP hosted the first of these. Traditionally, each of the four weekend races consisted of a doubles surfboat race, a half-mile swim, and a

103

singles surfboat race. This year, *Murphy's Tavern* held the after-the-race party, to which all thirteen beach patrols were invited, and enticed to show up by the offer of "your first drink free." As expected, it turned into a rowdy, beer-drinking event.

Most of the thirteen beach patrol guards, and especially some of their captains, took great pride in their team's performance. Wildwood BP was a bit of an exception to this phenomenon. On some of the other beach patrols star athletes rarely sat the lifeguard stand and did little real lifeguarding, but rather they would have the better part of their "work" day to work out at their specialty. This year, one such beach patrol, Avalon BP had won the Wildwood South Jersey Invitational, and, in *Murphy's Tavern,* fueled by the suds, they had their cackles up and began chanting, "We're number one. We're number one." The Wildwood lads had done even worse than usual, coming in dead last. So, not to be outdone, and outnumbering the Avalon boasters there in the bar by four to one, the Wildwood lads drowned out the "Number one" guys, with their own chant that went, "We're number thirteen. We're number thirteen." And, as superior as the race winners felt a moment ago, that's how daunted they were now, being overwhelmed by the sheer numbers disadvantage. To the Wildwood guys the races were a social event, a time to reconnect with friends from other beach patrols. There certainly was no shame in not excelling in ocean events that had little bearing on real lifeguard skills. When would a pair of lifeguards have to row at full tilt for a mile to make a rescue? That'd be a job for the Coast Guard. Or, a swimmer having to swim a quarter of a mile to reach a person in trouble? Long before that, a surfboat would have already been launched.

Sunday, July 11th
Sacrilege and retribution...

The next morning, Captain Capacio got a strange call, "Cap Capacio, this is Al Hastings, captain of the Stone Harbor Beach Patrol. It seems that after your tournament, one of your surfboats ended up on one of our beaches." The beach town of Stone Harbor was about eight miles north of Wildwood, however, just a five-mile row on the open ocean. Guessing what had happened, Captain Capacio stifled his chagrin. "No doubt, some exuberant, beer-fueled lifeguards had misappropriated one of our boats." For decades these surfboats had been lovingly produced by just a few boat craftsmen, Van Dyne and Van Zandt, so there attached to them a bit of reverence. To steal a beach patrol's surfboat was tantamount to horse thieving. But, which beach patrol guards had done it? Obviously, the perpetrators wouldn't have left the "evidence" on their own beachfront. But, who had done it? Ah ha, there *had* been a fly on the wall at *Murphy's* the night of the races, one Alfie Henderson, who was working the door that night. On his way to the head, he overheard the Avalon guards making the boast that they were going to co-opt a Wildwood surfboat and row it to their beach. In all likelihood, the "We're number thirteen" cheer didn't

105

sit too well with them. At work that morning, the theft of the Wildwood surfboat was all the buzz, and with the detective work of Alfie Henderson, the offenders were identified.

Now, for a plan...

Given gravity of the offence, full participation was all-but guaranteed. A sacrilege had been committed, and this called for redress. All hands, except for Captain Capacio, of course, because of his official status, were called to battle stations. *Murphy's Tavern,* Sunday night at nine was nominated to be the meeting place and time, appropriate since this had been the scene of the crime's origin. Five cars, with Lieutenant Shelly's van at the vanguard led the caravan. The marauders first stopped at beach HQ to pick up thirty pairs of nine-foot oars and boat plugs for the job. The venture nearly failed when the North Wildwood police, two summer cops, pulled Shelly's van over and looked in the back and saw all those oars, no doubt suspecting that they were possibly stolen. Fortunately, Shelly's badge and authoritarian manner carried the day, or, rather, the night. Arriving in Avalon, several dozen off-duty WBP lifeguards stealthily strode onto the desolate beach and righted a dozen surfboats, dragged them to the water's edge, and launched them for what had by now become a midnight row. Spirits in all twelve boats were buoyant for all hands in on the caper, that is, until they approached the treacherous shoals of Herford Inlet, whose confluence of strong ocean currents produces a formidable mile of wild white-water. Somewhat

106

miraculously, not a boat foundered. With just a few hundred yards after that riotous stretch of ocean, the twelve surfboats were beached at North Wildwood. Covertly, at the preordained street head, all thirty oarsmen were picked up without arousing suspicion, at what was now 3 a.m.

Monday, July 12th
The light of day…

Predicable to all except Captain Capacio himself, the call came in crisply at eight-thirty, "Cap, this is Captain Black of North Wildwood Beach Patrol; there are twelve Avalon surfboats beached here, out front on the sand. Would you have any information about this?" In a millisecond Cap sussed what had happened. And, with a mixture of both pride and annoyance, he feigned ignorance of the whole matter. Later that morning Cap called Lieutenant Shelly into his office and demanded, "Shelly, what do you know about his surfboat incident with Avalon?" After a stern minute of silence and with the office door safely secured, they both broke up in laughter. Cap never really did like the blustery captain of Avalon Beach Patrol, Murray Lupe, and now, while safely at arms' length, this really put it in his face.

Running on Empty
Jackson Browne

Only halfway into the summer, the late hours were starting to show on some of the guards. Around this time, Captain Capacio would do his "slow belt" talk at morning muster. The allusion, no doubt, had its origin in the former times when Philadelphia was a booming factory town with many a conveyor belt speeding production. With Cap's admonition that "Some of you need to get on the slow belt," he focused his words on Clem, *the Clam,* who, this morning came to work with a bad case of *thrush,* a fungal infection of the mouth that can set up when people get very run-down. To the amusement of all in the locker room, there was no doubt as to the source of Clem the Clam's malady. Clem had no doubt run into a "bad clam."

Fortunately, for Clem, *and* Ryan, as well by association, Clem could still blow his whistle, which meant that the thrush didn't keep him from work. That was the extent of it, though. He couldn't talk normally, so Ryan had to conduct all of the social interviews with the beach honeys. Some of them would ask, "Doesn't he talk?" In about a week or so the problem had cleared up and the boys had a good laugh when they remembered "the lifeguard and his mute stand partner" episode.

Monday night, July 12th
Heaven Must Be Missing an Angel
Tavares

With the drinking age at just eighteen in 1976, the Slippery Rock girls were out at the bars almost every night. By mid-June, they were working on perfect attendance at their favorite bar, the *Fairview*, where, on Mondays there was *Beat-the-Clock* night. Doors opened at nine to a boisterous crowd, anxious to get in on that first hour of the cheapest drinks of the night. Every hour the prices would edge upward, so that urged on by "the deal," the revelers were fairly wasted by midnight. Back at the apartment, the girls had vowed to "stay together," a move that guys commonly called "cock-blocking." Somehow or other, Jan went missing, the compact, no doubt, had slipped her mind. She and Alfie's stand partner, the rookie, Jeff had been dancing every song, and really hitting it off. Before too long, "Let's go outside to get a little fresh air," led to, Jeff's saying "Let's go back to my place for a little while." Jeff had won her over with a seductive argument that he thoroughly believed in. He had told her, "You know, Jan, we can have a whole lot of fun in bed without actually *doing it.* If we were to do it, it'd be because you told me that you wanted to. You're in charge." Jan liked Jeff's low-pressure, easy manner, as well as his persuasive blue eyes. "OK, we can go back to your place for a *little* while. I don't want the girls worrying about me."

Jeff's assurances had fit right in with Jan's outlook on sex. Although still a virgin at nineteen, she was of the Bill Clinton school of thought when it came to sex, that is, that only screwing was sex. Everything else, of course, preserved a girl's chastity. So, it turned out that the two had a wonderful time, until three in the morning that night at Jeff's place defending virginity.

Tuesday, July 13th
Listen to What the Man Said
   Paul McCartney & Wings

Walt the Salt had called down to the next stand to have Harry's rookie Steve to "cover" his stand while he went back to the toilet. When Walt got back, Steve stayed a while for a little conversation, which got around to Walt telling him, "Yeah, a few years ago I made the mistake of inviting my Colorado winter girlfriend to come visit me here during the summer. She did and stayed a week, a week too long, as it turned out. By August, when she arrived, I was juggling a half a dozen honeys, so having a girlfriend in town, especially one who knew no one else here and depended solely on me for company every minute, didn't play out too well. By day five she was seething and neither of us could wait until day seven, her departure day, came. I'll tell ya, I never again experimented with importation." Seasoned guards knew that having a steady girlfriend at the beach, even if for just a week, would be like, as they would say, "bringing a ham sandwich to the banquet."

A trip to the city…

Most guards on their days off do the busman's holiday, that is, they come to the beach. But, Ferris, Trashman, that is, on his day off, Wednesday, last week went home to see his five brothers and sisters and his parents. With his trip to the city, he saw the opportunity to get his laundry done, a chore that lifeguards often can't find the time to do. Ferris had a few substantial meals that only a mom could make, a good night's sleep, and he was back on the stand with Bobby the next morning.

The following Saturday at the beach he noticed his thirteen year old sister, Karen, coming down the beach toward his stand, and she seemed to be really stirred up. Before she got to even ten feet away she blurted out, "You pig, you gave Mommy the crabs!" How embarrassing for the kid up there on the lifeguard stand, amid loads of bathers on their beach chairs and blankets! Actually, though, in all likelihood, Ferris had been given the crabs, as well.

One of the drawbacks of communal "living" was that some rather unpleasant conditions were shared, like body lice, aka, "the crabs" and athlete's feet. Several times in the course of the summer when there erupted an outbreak of crabs in the guards' lockers, Captain Capacio would issue the edict that all lockers were to be cleaned out and that the guards take all of their gear and clothes home and wash them. This being done, the empty lockers would be fumigated. This might happen once or twice a summer. Oh, well, just the hazards of the job.

Wednesday, July 14th
Rock the Boat
The Hughes Corporation
Today, on the two-mile run of beach to the south and adjacent to Wildwood by the Sea calamity ruled. Despite the small-craft warnings, strong winds, and the six-foot seas, the captain of the Wildwood Crest Beach Patrol stuck to his immutable rule of "boats out" for boat patrol from two until four every day. Martinet that he was, Captain Hobson invariably paid no heed to prevailing ocean conditions. Rather than look at the ocean, he would look at his watch for a determination. Today, two surfboats on different beaches had capsized amid hordes of bathers. In one instance the crew had unwittingly let their surfboat fly down a breaking wave into a dense group of bathers. Once the lifeguard, sitting in the bow seat and who was on the oars lost control of the surfboat it was like being at the pinnacle of a willy-nilly rollercoaster, beginning its wild descent down the rails. Invariably, a loud, "Oh, shit!" from the bow man signaled impending calamity. The loud screams heard in this case were quite similar to that of the rollercoaster, except that in this scenario they were coming from *outside* of the "ride," that is, they were coming from the bathers who were being set upon by this 400-pound surfboat lurching intently toward them.

On other days, with strong offshore winds, the lifeguards of Wildwood Crest would spend most of their boat time at sea fighting their way back into position, so as to be in visual contact with the bathers. Wildwood guards, amused by Hobson's daily edict of "boats out from two to four," and by the fact that Hobson's "boat patrol" cut in half the number of guards sitting the stands, they scoffingly suggested that sending the guards to an afternoon happy hour would be just as effective as boat patrol in these unfavorable ocean conditions--this, because, if you were to need back-up manpower help with rescues, a boat couldn't be beached in any less than ten minutes, through a dense crown of bathers.

On the beach in Wildwood the boats were utilized more judiciously. For instance, in a situation in which there is a deep outside gully a long way off of the tide line, two guards sitting boat patrol can place their surfboat in close proximity to the gully bathers and hover effectively close, should a bather need assistance. Most rescues develop in either one of two ways. Usually bathers get drifted down-water by the prevailing south current that runs through the gullies. When they find themselves in water where they can no longer touch the bottom, then their swim test begins. If it becomes apparent to the lifeguard that they aren't going to swim out of danger and toward the shore, then the lifeguards swing into action.

The other scenario requiring a rescue typically comes about later in the summer season. South Atlantic storms intensify ocean currents, often cutting breaks in sandbars. As water brought shoreward by waves seeks its course of least resistance seaward, the water rushes out through

113

these breaks, creating riptides, or in South Jersey lifeguard parlance, "washes." Even very able swimmers are no match for washes, once caught in them. The trick, as smart ocean lifeguards well know, is to swim to the left or right of the wash, parallel to the shoreline and then to return to land, while swimming back in over unbroken lengths of the sandbar.

The Spotlight...

Not all good pals who were veteran guards asked to sit the stand together. Peter O'Neill, originally a Philly boy, who now spent winters out in Steamboat, Colorado as a ski instructor, and Gary Lieber, better known by his beach name, "Seadog," were good friends. This summer they were sitting stands #10 and #11. Actually, they had requested stands *next* to each other. Although, before the summer had begun, Peter had said to Gary, "Hey, why don't you and I sit together? We both have the rap and it would make setting up dates with girls a lot easier." But, Seadog resisted, saying, "No, I like it a lot better sitting stands *next* to each other," never offering any further rationale. Peter had always found *Seadog's* reluctance to sitting on the same stand a bit of a mystery, but didn't push the subject any further. He speculated that perhaps Seadog didn't want to share the spotlight when it came to talking with beach honeys.

There were benefits, though, to sitting on adjacent lifeguard stands, in that it was somewhat relaxing to have someone good on the stand next to you, since having a very able guard there eased the work it would have entailed should the guard on the next stand have been at all sketchy. With a solid, experienced guard at the next stand, you wouldn't have to watch their water and call their rescues for them. Also, this arrangement gave them double coverage with the honeys, especially the ones who would only walk down to the water and then back to their blanket. If either of the boys met a prospective pair of cuties, he'd just whistle down to the other that he was sending down a couple of girls to be met.

Depending on who had first met the girls, the other lifeguard would give the young ladies a brief build-up of the other. "Yeah, he's a really nice guy. He's a junior in college and a lot of fun. (A line that either one would say, referring to the other.) Just take a walk down and say 'Hello.' I've whistled down to him that you are on your way to meet him. I'm sure you'll like him. He's a nice, easygoing guy." It was their standard operating procedure, with Peter and Gary always nominating an eight o'clock rendezvous. "Eight o'clock" would give the boys time to shower up and get over to the *Terminal Bar* for a few beers before meeting their dates.

Thursday, July 15th

Every morning before sending half the crew out to their stands and the other half to their workouts, Captain Capacio held a morning briefing, mainly to get all the lads minds refocused on the job at hand, lifeguarding. Routinely, he would say, "OK, you pretty boys hiding in the back, get in closer and listen up." After pertinent subjects like tide changes, weather, and the beaches with riptide potential were covered, Cap turned his attention to Harry. "Harry, we had a local woman call in yesterday saying that you had stopped and talked to forty-five different girls." Evidently, this local biddy, with nothing better to do, had seen first-hand just how effectively "the funnel" worked. "No, Cap, that lady's mistaken." Then, after a slight pause that silenced everyone in the locker room, "Cap, it was really forty-seven." Everyone broke up at this. Even Captain Capacio had to suppress his laughter. Then, Harry, so as to not appear insolent, added, "Cap, I promise to scale it way back today." The badinage had really lightened the mood of the briefing and all the boys filed out for another day's work at the beach in great spirits.

Later in the day...

On the stand, late in the afternoon, Jeff asked Alfie, "How have you gotten off to lifeguard these last 11 years?" "Well, when I first got on the guards, I was going to college, studying something that I thought would get me into a profession, one at which I might make good money. So, I was studying business. Then, one rainy day during that first summer, I came across a *Sports Illustrated* article about this guy who was eighty-four and still lifeguarding the ocean in, I think it was, Far Rockaway, New York. And, I was really struck by something that he said in the article, which was, 'After that first summer lifeguarding on the ocean I decided that I would have to work at something that would give me summers off for the rest of my life. So, I went into teaching.'

116

"And, that's exactly what *I* did. On one of my days off from the beach, I went up to college and changed my major from business to education. In my senior year I was lucky enough to get assigned to do my student teaching in a very upscale high school outside of Philly, at Glenside Prep. When I graduated, they offered me a full-time position, and I've been there ever since. Looking back, choosing education made all the difference. I would have been a very unhappy bean-counter."

While Jeff had gotten Alfie into a talkative mood, Alfie recalled some of the funny stuff that had happened during his time on the beach. One story that he remembered was, "There were years when some of the rookies who came to be Wildwood lifeguards had, up to that point, led somewhat sheltered lives. This would become readily apparent in the showers. Since the guards showered around a central post with four or five spouts, the activity was anything but private. The shy ones had a few ploys in trying to conceal their reluctance to shower with the boys. Some would wait until just about all the guards were finished and then sneak in for a very brief shower. Others were even more conspicuous, in that they'd wear a swimsuit into the showers.

"From time to time, I had some good fun with these shy guys. Sometimes, I'd see them alone in the shower and I'd walk in with my shampoo in one hand and my towel in the other, all the while having my big yellow comb there in my pubes. What a look of both embarrassment and disgust when they finally got around to spotting the comb. Better yet

117

was the time after work that I had been pitching softball warm-ups too close to this guy named Piez, who I later learned had been All-Catholic in both baseball and football. He stung a line drive and it caught me right in the privates. The next day and for about ten days afterward my whole dick and scrotum turned pitch black. With this one, I'd sidle into the shower with my back to the victim, engage them in a little conversation, and, then I'd turn to face them. In short order their gaze would drift downward and spot this horrible black mass. 'Yikes!' The reaction was much better than with 'the comb.' Very often they'd run right out of the shower, even with the shampoo suds still in their hair."

Friday, July 16th
(I'm just a) Love Machine
   The Miracles
         Backed up already at 7 o'clock in *Jersey Shore* Friday night traffic, three young brewery workers, Gail, Hope, and Ruth from Reading, Pa. obliviously rattled on about past adventures with the lifeguards of Wildwood by the Sea. All three were in their early-twenties and rather attractive, as well. The lifeguards loved them, or, rather, love to see them back in town. Gail gushed, "I can't wait to see those beautiful guys sitting up there on their lifeguard stands in those tight little *Speedos.*" 'Wow, I can't wait," agreed Ruth. The ladies just loved that those skimpy little nylon bathing suits left little to the imagination. The "package," as they called it, was clearly displayed, with all its sensuous contours and

118

outlines. "I don't know about you girls, but I'm getting wet just talking about it," from Ruth.

The trio was quite a team. Groups of lifeguards would invite them over to their places and after their arrival; one by one the guys would migrate to their bedrooms with one of the ladies and get right down to business. Gail, the wildest of the lot would actually climax while giving oral sex. Yes, sir, the guards always gave them a big welcome on their frequent sojourns to *the Shore.*

The ladies arrived a bit late this Friday night, ten o'clock, but no matter. The bars wouldn't close until two. And, they did have a good idea of where to find some of the Wildwood lifeguards hanging out. The ladies routinely stayed at the *Atlantic Star*, an old-time wooden rooming house back near the bay and about as far from the beach as one could get. Just like in *Monopoly,* the board game, the farther from Boardwalk in the beach town of Wildwood, the cheaper the hotel rates. The *Atlantic Star* was one of those three-story, firetrap dives where boarders often paid for a room on the premise of there being only two of them and then packing in six or eight. In the case of these girls the opposite often held true.

Gail had said, in fact, "This room is just a place to keep our stuff, shower, and head back out. The less we see of this room, the better time we'll have." Hope and Ruth beamed in agreement, since, with these girls, that was entirely true. They would pay the *Atlantic Star* for three to the room, and more often than not, none of them would make it home for the night, all three having found mates for the night.

119

After the few minutes it took to freshen up from the long drive, they were ready to go. "Let's get going and find the lifeguards and some good company for the night." It didn't matter which of the ladies had said it, the three were all of one mind when it came to men.

Sunday, July 18th

When Will I See You Again
  The Three Degrees

For weeks now Alfie had been trying to connect with Stephanie, the New York girl whith whom he had hooked up with at the *Southwind* "Spin the Wheel," but she was always out when he called, and since *he* had no phone there at *the Shore,* there was no number for her at which to call him back. Then one morning at roll call at the beach headquarters Captain Capacio called Alfie to the phone. Stephanie's voice brought an immediate smile to his face. "Yes, that would be great. This weekend?" The sheik denizens of New York City were to arrive Friday night and Stephanie hinted, "And, I think that we'll have an even better time when we see each other again," certainly piquing Alfie's interest and curiosity, since he thought to himself, *How could we possibly have a better time than we had had on Stephanie's last visit.*

Hillary and Stephanie loved their upscale Manhattan life. They worked as legal secretaries for the same high-powered law firm, which had its own wellness center and as a perk to their positions, the girls were given five hours release-time during the work week to workout, time that they fully utilized on the elliptical machines, the aerobics classes, and the weight machines. No wonder those splendid twenty-two year old bodies. Work ended loosely around five and merged invariably with happy hour on the trendy Upper East Side. Most of the happening, after-work bars were within a five-minute walk. And, it goes without saying; these two stars rarely had to pay for their drinks.

Part of the reason it was so hard for Stephanie and her South Jersey lifeguard, Alfie, to reach each other on the phone, was that by the time she and Hillary got off the Staten Island Ferry and drove to their apartments, Alfie was lost in space, amid the Wildwood nightlife. Often, in between dry *Boodles* gin Martinis, Stephanie would say to Hillary, "You know, I've really got to get in touch with that good-looking lifeguard, Alfie. So, what do you say, Hill, let's do plan to get back down to *the Shore* soon again" Then, from across the bar a young executive-type would catch their eye and mouth, "Would you like another drink, ladies?" Two sweet smiles of "Yes" naturally followed, making *the Shore* too distant a concept to consider at the moment.

What the unsuspecting benefactor across the bar didn't know was that he had been selected by the ladies beforehand to buy their next round of drinks. Hillary and Stephanie were so good at it that they made a game of being able to choose which guy would be next. Together they would choose a dupe, make eye contact with him, and then flash those alluring smiles of theirs, and bingo, two more drinks were on their way. To them, they were just

121

demonstrating their sexual power over men. They had it and they loved it.

At the beach…

Clem the Clam, now fully recovered from his bout with the *thrush*, and Dunes, Ryan had hit the jackpot yesterday at the beach, two nurses from Pittsburgh, Clare and Sue, down for a long weekend. They had been out to the bars last night, their first night in town and had expressed to the lads that they had found the crowd a "little too young." Sensing opportunity, Dunes had asked, "What do you ladies have planned for tonight?" "Oh, we thought that we might go on the rides," Clare said. In unison and, no doubt, from lots of practice, the boys responded, "The rides? *We're* the rides!" The ladies laughed, but were definitely interested. The time to meet was set at seven, and, of course, the meeting place was the *Keg Bar.* Luckily, this time there was no need for the "wait until the boss comes in to cash our checks" ruse. The ladies were flush and insisted on treating the drinks "for you two poor lifeguards." By nine, after lots of beers for the boys and grasshoppers for the nurses, the couples were off to Clem the Clam's crib.

Then today, at around two, Clem spotted the girls coming their way from about two stands away. As they got closer, they looked to have something "up their sleeve." "How are you ladies today" Ryan offered. "Not too well," said Clare." "Oh, how's that?" from Ryan. "Well, we want a refund. We didn't like 'the rides' last night." It seems that after all the drinks at the *Keg* both Clem and Ryan had fallen asleep on the girls before any romance had taken place. After some embarrassed chuckles and apologies, the boys were issued a second chance, giving them the chance to reclaim their good reputations. During the next three remaining nights, before the ladies left for their drive back home to Pittsburgh, they were quite satisfied the these boys *were,* in fact, "the rides."

Captain Capacio,
Wildwood Beach Patrol, 1941-1977

To date, Captain Capacio, (affectionately known to the guards as just "Cap"), the man in charge of this menagerie, had been associated with the Beach Patrol for over 35 years. Despite standing only five-feet-seven, Cap had a huge bearing. With well-furrowed Mediterranean skin, Cap would rarely be seen without his signature *Parodi* Italian stogie. One could immediately discern the wisdom residing behind those ageless, unflinching eyes. From the age of seventeen until the time of this story, with the exception of his four-year U.S Navy service during World War II, he had sat the lifeguard stand, became a lieutenant, and eventually captain. Most of the lads in his charge felt lucky to have such loyal and understanding man at the helm.

Part of the explanation for Captain Capacio's forgiving nature toward his wards, the lifeguards, was that he had been a lifeguard himself. And, in rare moments, at his favorite after-the-beach hangout, the American Legion on Pacific Avenue, he had told "his boys" stories of how he and his close buddy, Juvinal, had often gone up to Atlantic City where the bars were open all night, only to return to Wildwood in the wee hours of the morning. And, so as not to be late for work after staying up all night, they'd sleep right there on the ramp to the beach headquarters. So, Cap knew first-hand what it was like to be a Wildwood lifeguard.

When occasionally a guard had conspicuously continued the boozing until it became time for work, Cap would simply tell him, "Go home and sleep it off. You've been working hard these last few months and could use an extra day off." Or, when a guard came to work, unbeknownst to himself, with half of his face body-painted, Cap would simply bring him over to the mirror, have a good laugh with the guard, and a face-washing would resolve the matter. On other beach patrols these lifeguards would have, no doubt, faced disciplinary action, or even been fired. One of the few times Cap was backed into a corner and had no recourse but to fire a lifeguard was with a guard named Lou Celluci, who, owing to his body shape, was called "the Plum." He persistently showed up for work late. At one point, Cap even bought him an alarm clock. It didn't have any effect. So, eventually, Cap had to let him go.

The Plum had another descriptive nickname, "Lock'em up Lou," attributed to his pugnacious penchant for starting fights with male bathers. Where a simple explanation of the beach rules would have settled matters, the Plum would start right off yelling at people, and then he would invoke his quasi-police authority to arrest the guys. So, without it ever

124

having to be discussed among the Wildwood lifeguards, they all felt that the patrol was better off without the Plum.

Another example of Cap's leniency toward his men came when, Alfie Henderson, after working the patrol for a few years as Bob McConnolly, came to Cap with a fishy story, "Cap, when I was younger, my mother remarried and now my legal name has been changed to Alfie Henderson." The real story was that when Alfie had signed on to the beach patrol, he was met with a dilemma. As a guard he would clear but forty-seven dollars a week, whereas, at the time was he receiving forty-five dollars a week in unemployment compensation. In effect, Alfie would be making only two dollars a week more to take the job as a lifeguard. The resolution came when a good friend, the *real* Bob McConnolly, who then was working off the books, aka, "under the table," suggested that Alfie use his name and social security number. In the beginning, it took a while for Alfie to get used to being "Bobby," but after a while the guards knew him only as Bobby. Years later, the real McConnoly went legitimate and had to recover his own name and social security number, telling Alfie, "Hey, pal, I hate to tell you this, but, now I have a real job, making good money, and I have to ask you to stop using my name and social security number." Showing just how lenient a boss Cap was; when met with "Bobby's" sketchy reasoning, Cap just knitted his eyebrows and already sensing the answer, asked, "Now, if anyone should come around and ask if this guy McConnoly ever worked the beach patrol, what

125

do I say?" Although Cap had obviously smelled a rat, the matter was quickly dismissed, with a knowing smile from the boss.

Monday, July 19th
Get Down on It
Kool & the Gang

The brewery girls, Gail, Hope, and Ruth from Reading, Pa. had had a fantastic weekend, having been hosted by five different housefuls of Wildwood lifeguards. Lots of beer, lots of laughs, and, of course, lots and lots of sex. The bedrooms had had revolving doors. And, true to reputation, Gail did climax giving head. Often the favored lifeguard had to suppress a giggle as she got down on it, and even while sucking it, from time to time, she would moan a crescendo of, "Oh, oh, oh…" with her eyes rolled back, searching the heavens in ecstasy each time she repeatedly climaxed. Her attention to an erection bordered on reverence; the phallus put her into a trance-like state. To the boys delight, she was insatiable. One after another, a guard would emerge from the room and say, "Who wants to be next?"

On Saturday night, the inevitable came about. Clem the Clam happened to be over at a lifeguard house where the brewery ladies were playing "musical beds," when one of the resident guys introduced Clem to Gail. Once in the bedroom, no time was wasted in preliminaries like foreplay. It took but a minute in the bedroom for them to realize that here was perfection. Each of them had met their match in their devotion to oral sex, while at the same time having their own genitals sublimely catered to.

126

Time passed by quickly and, their door didn't open until four hours later, around midnight.

Late Sunday night, before their northbound Chrysler reached mile ten on the Garden State Parkway they were contriving their next getaway to *the Shore.* Comparing notes among themselves on their way home, there were lots of shared juicy details, details that would certainly stay hushed and guarded once they were back in Reading, Pa.

Back to the brewery on Monday, the ladies had a hard time coming down from such an erotic weekend. For the first few days, they'd meet up after work at the *Grog Shoppe,* an upscale local bar, where they'd find a remote booth, out of earshot of other bar patrons. There, they would decompress over a few rounds of beers, rattle on at high speed about their past-weekend exploits with "the boys," reliving the exciting times that they had had at *the Shore.* For Gail readjustment was the worst. At work, it was an itch that had to be relieved, which she did with frequent trips to the employees' lavatory. Once there, she'd go into one of the stalls, lock the door, drop her panties, and treat her pussy to ten minutes on the vibrator. To fellow workers who afterward would perhaps notice it, she'd explain away her glassy eyes with, "Oh, I think I'm getting the flu."

I'll call you later, after the beach.

Jan, the sweet cheerleader of the Slippery Rock girls, had a unique attribute that facilitated her getting together with lifeguard Jeff several nights a week. She had something that only the rarest few summer people back then had. She had a landline telephone in her room at their apartment. Today, it may be hard to imagine a time when people weren't in immediate contact. In those days, phone companies were leery of summer residents, who often skipped out on their final month's bill. They therefore required documentation of year-round residency. Jan, realizing the social value of having a phone, prevailed on their kindly landlady to take responsibility for the bill. Jan convincingly assured her that she would faithfully settle her final phone bill at the end of the summer.

I'd Really Love to See You Tonight
England Dan and John Ford Coley

On nights when nothing had materialized with honeys on the beach that day, Jeff would give Jan a call at around seven. "Hi Jan, what are you doing tonight?" he'd ask. "Mmm, why?" She didn't want to appear too ready. "I thought we might get together," from Jeff. "OK, Jeff, how about eight?" This tacit arrangement allowed them both a bit of freedom and latitude. Jeff had a cozy little apartment back on the bay, where they spent many enjoyable nights together. Jan did, though, have one slightly irksome proviso: "Jeff, as you know, I do have to be home before dawn." This, of course, was in line with her "good girl" concept of herself. "I like to get ready for work and be able to bike to work with my roommates." Jeff kiddingly would say, "You know that Beach Boys' song, *Wouldn't It Be Nice,* that's our song." The gist of the song was that it'd be great if they could kiss "goodnight" and stay together

128

rather than having to part company in the wee hours of the morning. Nonetheless, Jan's sweet company overruled any slight perturbations that the early twilight drive home entailed.

Trouble in Paradise...

With Jan's roommate, Betsy, all wasn't going so well. No one had to tell her, the most outgoing of the Slippery Rock girls, to slow down. Missing her period had done that. After two weeks of great anxiety, she finally brought herself to overcome the embarrassment of asking the pharmacist for a pregnancy test. To her greatest relief, the test proved negative. Too close a call not to modify her sexual behavior for the remainder of the summer. From then on, she demanded that the boys use condoms, and if they were brainless enough not to have them, she did.

Tuesday, July 20th
Bad Blood
Neil Sedaka & Elton John

Alfie, in his 11 years on the patrol had come to know the politics of the Wildwood BP, as well as that of the surrounding beach patrols, and today on the stand he was filling Jeff in on some of the inner workings, saying, "For some reason, probably attributable to the fact that Captain Capacio is a very down-to-earth guy with lots of life experiences, and having been on the guards from back in the forties, our patrol has often been a refuge for lifeguards who had run into trouble on other beach patrols. Usually the prior offences were of the nature of rowdy behavior, often having been fired for being part of a bar fight or some other public disturbance. No doubt, Cap had seen or been involved in a few these sort of fracases himself during his four-year tour in the navy, and knew that the combatants were generally good guys who had just gotten fired up on a bit too much booze. Invariably, given the second chance, these past miscreants had learned their lessons and had settled down, and, now were no more of a problem than any other of our lifeguards.

"Not all of these transfer guards had been the source of the trouble. A good case in point was Gary Lieber, Seadog, who sits stand # 11 with second-year guard, Charley Booth. To hear Gary, himself, tell it, he'd say, 'Yeah, I'd been chased off the Wildwood Crest BP because, at 23, I had become too old in the eyes of the then man in charge, Captain Joe Freeland.' Alfie continued, "By reputation, Freeland was a bit of a Captain Queeg character, the captain in the *Caine Mutiny*. Freeland often put as many as half the lifeguards from a previous season on the 'do not rehire list,' using their age as the sole disqualification for rehire. Gary had told us, 'For days on end, Freeland would park his beach patrol vehicle a few yards behind my stand and openly make notes about me. It was pretty unnerving, putting up with Freeland's head games day after day. Finally I got the message.' The following summer, Wildwood BP, in person of Gary Lieber, added a very skillful lifeguard and all-around good guy to the roster."

Heading west…

This morning, the Pittsburgh nurses, Clare and Sue began their eight-hour drive west on I-70. Over the last eight years they had become close friends. In the beginning they knew each other by name only. Before political correctness had seized the land, scores for college exams were posted by students' names, and Clare and Sue's names consistently appeared in the top three of their one-hundred-and-eighty student anatomy and physiology lecture classes at the Penn State satellite campus in Beaver County. Only later, when they both took the elective class, *Total Fitness,* while in nursing school at the main campus at University Park did they get to meet and become friends.

They laughed once again when they recounted how each of them, unknowingly to the other, had used their sexual wiles on their professor of the *Total Fitness* course, the rakish professor, Doctor Feehan. Clare, a pretty blonde coed had turned in her first exam of the course, and then walked over to Dr. Feehan and put her arm around his shoulder and asked in a sweet voice, "Professor, What was the answer to number *three,* please?" while aspirating a light puff of air into his ear on the word "three*.* " Sue had taken a different tack in getting the professor's attention. She had visited him during his regular office hours, feigning difficulty with some physiological process. Her ploy was to bring her chair right next to his, while "accidentally" rubbing her knee against his several times during his explanations. In the ensuing weeks of the course, Dr. Feehan often had trouble staying on his notes, with these two lovelies consistently sitting in the first row of his classroom.

Wednesday, July 21ˢᵗ

On this rare foul-weather day at the beach, on stand # 4, Harry, the vet, at twenty-six and Steve, the rookie were having a very pointed conversation, the provocation of which being that Steve, at the tender age of twenty was planning to get engaged that fall. Harry, a pure skeptic, had been through any number of winter girlfriends, the dénouement of which had always and eventually come with the start of another summer *on the wood.* Harry liked to say, "They meet you, they like you, then the renovations begin. First you need to get a better car. *I'm embarrassed to be seen in that car of yours.* But, not only a better car but better friends, too. Eventually, she'll get around to disliking all of *your* guy friends, especially the single ones. Before too long, you'll find that the only guys that you're having conversations with are the husbands of *her* friends, with whom, for the most part, you have nothing in common. Also, as part of the general reconstruction of you, she'll begin to dress you like the doll, Ken of *Ken and Barbie.* She'll go through all of your clothes and decide what's to be kept and what's to be thrown out."

Harry summed it up by asking Steve, "Who does it benefit, marriage, that is?" "Both," was Steve's response. "Well, I'll tell you what, kid, when you go home tonight and have a little quiet time, make up two lists. On one write what she will gain by marriage, on the other what you will gain. I think that after giving the matter some honest thought, hers will be a rather long one, while yours will be very short. And, if you wrote on yours 'regular sex' forget it. That was just the bait to trip you into marriage. Remember the old joke, 'Why is the bride smiling so broadly in the wedding pictures?' The answer of course is no more blow jobs! It's like buying on the installment plan. Let's say a guy buys a TV on a three-year payment schedule, and that by two years the TV is nothing but static, *but* he's still paying on it. That's marriage!" Then, Harry added, "There used to be an old Irish bar owner here in town named Paddy Ward, who liked to say, 'Love is blind, but marriage is a real eye-opener.'"

Harry was a bit of a chauvinist, no doubt. Another pet peeve of his was, as he put it, "People using the term, 'womanizer,' especially when a guy uses it. It is, after all, a term of social disapproval intended to keep men in line, that is, monogamous." If used at all among the lifeguards (which it probably wouldn't be) it'd be a laudable comment. Harry would say, "Extended monogamy is just an unnatural state, and ocean lifeguarding on the beach here in Wildwood is the loophole by which to escape the trap." Even when people would point out couples to him that appeared to be relatively happy, Harry would throw up his hand, much as a traffic cop would do in halting traffic, and with great authority he'd say, "Just wait!" giving great emphasis to the "wait." Steve would laugh and say, "Harry you've been on the beach too long," whereas, Harry *knew* that Steve hadn't been on the beach long enough.

Tommy the beach cop…

Owing to the great number of beachgoers, especially on the weekends, the Wildwood by the Sea beach itself could occasionally grow unwieldy to manage. Rather than have the regular police bringing their ominous aura to the sand, WBP employed a few guys in white shirts and tee shirts that read "Beach Police." No guns, no clubs. Being basically a job in name only, there was very little accountability. They simply had to check in for roll call at the beginning of the day and check out at day's end. One of these characters, who for rather obvious reasons was called Tommy High, took full advantage of his relative invisibility. From two o'clock on, on most afternoons he could be found policing his gin and tonic at the *Surf Club* happy hour. His one identifiable duty was to take down the American flag on the beach when they played the national anthem at five every afternoon from speakers on the boardwalk. When Captain would get calls from the American Legion that the flag was still flapping in the wind at midnight, the matter would be sternly taken up with Tommy High the next morning. After several of these go-rounds, the flag pole mysteriously disappeared. And, remarkably, not another word was ever afterward said about it.

Another amusing anecdote involving Tommy High was this one. Often the beach cops got to discover situations that were called "land emergencies" before the guard on the stand did.

Broken arms, dislocated shoulders, arterial cuts (perhaps caused by a sharp broken clam shell) fell into this category of emergencies. The signal would then get sent to the nearest lifeguard stand by the beach cop who has come upon the emergency and then it would get passed from stand to stand by each lifeguard blowing repeated short blasts on his whistle while crossing and opening his arms overhead.

Profuse bleeding can be a serious issue at the beach. One day in June beach cop Tommy High called a land emergency. There certainly was heavy blood loss but when the jeep did arrive with its siren blasting, and a large crowd forming they were puzzled since there was no apparent victim, yet Tommy High seemed to be in quite a dither. In explaining the situation, he stuttered, "It's my girlfriend," which only added more confusion to the situation, "She's bleeding." In short order, it was revealed that there was in fact heavy bleeding, stemming from Tommy's girlfriend's monthly visitor. Thereafter, out at the bars, off-duty guards would often razz Tommy by imitating the land emergency signal, frantically waving their arms over their heads, and shouting, "She's bleeding, she's bleeding."

Friday, July 23rd

Hillary and Stephanie, the New York hotties, had executed their plan to weasel their way out of work on Friday, were through the Holland Tunnel by three, on the Garden State Parkway by four, and arrived in Wildwood at seven. Alfie had arranged to meet them in the lifeguard hangout, the *Terminal*

Bar, thinking, *There'd be a nice lineup of sun-tanned boys of summer, among which Hillary could choose, leaving Stephanie and me alone to our long-awaited get-together.*

Like most of the switched-on, more experienced lifeguards, Alfie wasted no time going home to clean up and get ready for Friday night, rather, he had showered at beach headquarters and was out "on the bricks" for the night at six. At the bar, before the New York ladies were to arrive, Alfie was saying to Walt the Salt, "You know, it's a curious phenomenon that some girls' stock goes way up when they're dressed up for the night out, just as other girls' stock takes a dive when dressed up for the night. And, as long as we have been working the beach we often overlook an average or even slightly homely face in a girl who has a kick-ass body, and on the other side of the coin, we might take no notice of a very pretty girl with just an average body." Then, with a twinge of pleasant reverie, Alfie thought to himself, *The New York girls, Hillary and Stephanie, are certainly the exception to the rule. They look sensational by day* and *by night.*

By six-thirty, more than a dozen guards had shown up at the *Terminal,* knocking back *Pabst Blue Ribbons* at five-for-a-dollar. Occasionally, a non-lifeguard friend or two of a lifeguard would show up at the bar and say, "Oh, I don't drink that cheap beer," to which Alfie and the lads would always say, "Here at the *Terminal* we don't drink adjectives, we just drink beer." At around seven, all eyes shot to the opening front door, through which two ravishing dolls emerged, Hillary and Stephanie. Most of Alfie's fellow guards hadn't seen the pair at the *Southwind* when the ladies were there some weeks ago, or had forgotten about them. Stephanie elicited quite a buzz when she cut right through the crowd to Alfie and bestowed on him a prolonged kiss. These girls had no shyness to them. Alfie found the ladies seats at the bar, and immediately they became the center of attention. After giving the bartender some brief instructions, the ladies had *Cosmopolitans,* shaken and strained, a welcome anodyne to their tedious, three-hour drive.

Alfie's scheme of hooking Hillary up with one of his mates at the *Terminal Bar* had begun to stall. Although Hillary acted pleasant and perky with the boys, nonetheless, she showed no special interest in any one of them in particular. Alfie began to worry that his and Stephanie's much-anticipated time together in bed might be in jeopardy, that they'd run out of time, since he knew that their last time in town the ladies had agreed to barhop every night together.

Time got away and sure enough at around nine Stephanie whispered to Alfie, "We're going back to the hotel, but why don't you come along with us." No problem. He was now guessing that if the three of them went out to the bars, *then* Hillary would either find a guy that she favored or that she'd simply release Stephanie to go off with Alfie. Although a bit frustrated that their romance had to be deferred slightly, Alfie knew that the wait would be handsomely rewarded. At the *Zephyr Motel,* with Hillary, demurely said, "Please excuse me for a

138

while, I need to shower. I won't be long." With this first opportunity to get really intimate since the girls had arrived in town, the lovers rekindled their ardor. Their passionate standing kiss quickly moved to the bed. *Maybe Hillary will go out on her own, after all,* Alfie thought, while at the same time worrying that she wouldn't and that tonight this brief interlude would be all that he and Stephanie would have.

This worry was instantly erased when the opening of the bathroom door momentarily drew Alfie's attention. There stood Hillary in just her bra and panties. She then revealed a little secret of theirs with, "Alfie, when we first saw you at the *Southwind Bar,* both Steph and I loved what we saw. But, since it was Steph that you came on to, we just let matters take their course. Then, on our ride back to New York after that weekend, Steph gave me all the sensuous details of your time together in bed. How you both enjoyed doing sixty-nine. And, as I now see, that you have a nice big dick. She got me wet just talking about it. So, good friend that Steph is, she freely agreed to let me in on the fun on our next trip to *the Shore.* I do hope you don't mind." And, with this, Hillary let her bra drop to the floor, exposing two dark brown, excited nipples. She walked over to Alfie, kissing him passionately, while sweetly stroking he already-stiff cock. Now, with the game plan in order, the trio moved to the bed. That night, with two delicious pussies, one very strong cock, and three willing mouths, the enjoyment was non-stop. All thoughts of the ladies going out on a bar hop that night were summarily dismissed. After

139

all, how could three people possibly have any more fun than this?

Saturday, July 24th

This sunny day, Walt the Salt, sitting stand # 3 had noticed that the rookie on stand # 4, Steve, had been talking to a beach honey for what seemed to be hours. She was becoming what the veteran lifeguards refer to as a "barnacle." With Steve's vet, Harry, away from the stand, Walt told his partner, "Hey, Sam I need to take a walk down and give the kid some advice." Once there, Walt climbed up the rungs and took his place next to Steve. Confidentially, he asked the rook, "Are you taking this honey out tonight?" Steve's reply was, "I haven't decided yet?" "So, why not?" "Well, I can't tell whether she'll be any action or not," Steve answered. Walt gave him a wry smile and said, "Do this. Get down off the stand and put your arm around her. If she pulls away, forget it. On the other hand, if she snuggles closer to you, you're in. It's that easy." Steve quickly found out that he was "in" if he wanted to be. Walt had seen many a young lifeguard talk endlessly to a honey at their stand, only to ruefully discover that she was a cold fish that night. In short order, Steve had garnered years of accumulated expertise.

Sunday, July 25th

The morning began beautifully, with a crystal clear sky and a lazy aquamarine ocean. Harry on stand # 4 had the early set-up and Steve would be down to the stand at around eleven, after the weekend CPR review and breakfast with the boys at the *Lanai Coffeeshop*. Harry loved getting to his lifeguard stand early, to a fairly desolate beach, and to see the day develop. With birds high aloft, riding thermals up into the wispy cirrus clouds above and fine weather in the offing, this day promised to be an especially good social one, since there would be a high-tide right around midday. The "funnel" would work especially well today. By noon, the lifeguard stand and the surfboat on its trailer would be right up there with the tourists' blankets and beach chairs, giving walkers (the girls, that is) no other option but to pass right in front of the stand. (On low-tide days, and with a fifty-yard differential between high and low tide, the walkers could be twenty or thirty yards away, should they walk behind the stand.)

With all of this temptation surrounding him, rookie Steve, with his impending fall engagement looming, was beginning to feel the noose tighten. Sitting with the "monogamy" skeptic, Harry, for a month now had shaken Steve's resolve a bit. Fueling the fire, as Harry well-knew, he'd frequently and sarcastically ask Steve, "Are you really getting *married?*" By now, Steve would inwardly shudder each time Harry would bring up the question. On more than a few occasions Steve had gone along with Harry when he had set up dates with honeys for the evening. Steve did have to admit to himself that these nights out were a lot of fun *and* that the ladies were quite good-looking and sexy. God forbid, though, were his fiancée, Lucy, to find out. Unnoticed by her, and fortunately for Steve, his excitement at the thought of her weekend visits had begun to wane. On one occasion, and, almost thinking out loud, Steve said, "Wow, it's Friday already." Harry just smiled, since he knew that there was a bit of dread betrayed in the statement, and that his sermons on the bachelor lifestyle were taking hold.

Monday, July 26th

As cushy as Tommy High had it with the beach cop job, he saw the spotlight that the guards enjoyed, up there on the wood, and although he wasn't much of a swimmer, he persuaded Cap to let him lifeguard. "Come on, Cap, I've been practicing. Alfie has been coaching me down at the borough pool and I think I can pass the swim test." So, although it had been a less than stellar finish for Tommy in his privileged, private swim test, he passed--*narrowly*. Once canonized, he was assigned to sit with Crazy Mike on stand #12, a quiet beach where most of the Wildwood bartenders, entertainers, and waitresses went to the beach. No accident that the boys were assigned this stand, on a beach where the likelihood of water action was indeed low.

This afternoon, Tommy, Crazy Mike, and six other guards from adjacent towers were called in on a chain rescue, one in which the lead lifeguard would put the victim on his Peterson buoy, followed in sequence by arriving guards swimming and extending their rescue buoys. The effect of which established a chain of some thirty feet of buoys and rope being pulled on, until the shore-most guards would be able to tug on the "chain" while standing up. Being a rather long rescue, it entailed a lot of hard swimming. On this one, Captain Capacio, himself, swam out to direct and assist. Immediately, he noticed a rather bizarre victim, one Tommy High. Thinking quickly, Cap ordered that this surprise victim take off his lifeguard redtop jersey, with its WBP lettering. Shameful it certainly would have been to have the large crowd of tourists that had gathered at the shoreline see a Wildwood Beach Patrol member being towed in as a victim. Since Tommy truly looked the part, while gasping for air, no one in the gathered crowd suspected otherwise.

Tuesday, July 27th
Kodachrome   **Paul Simon**

This day, a bit of sadness visited Alfie at stand # 7. Sandy, a very fit, tight-bodied twenty-two-year-old daily beach runner came by the stand. She had thoroughly loved her four summers at *the Shore* and was walking the beach and stopping by to bid adieu to a half dozen or so of the guards with whom at one time or another she had been intimate. For Sandy, the time had now come to "grow up." She had signed up for a four-year tour in the U.S. Army, and was leaving town that night. She had enjoyed having fun in bed just as much as the guys did, and no one ever talked about her behind her back, and, if anything, she was always treated as a pal by all the Wildwood lifeguards. Now, with Kodak in hand, she wanted one parting photo of herself and Alfie. Certainly, Alfie complied, having a friendly passer-by take a few shots. Alfie then said, "Hey, Sandy, I have an even better idea. Photos get lost but real memories last forever." At the time, a favorite summer tune was appropriately playing, Chicago's *Old Days*. Alfie turned the radio up and said, "Let's take a mental photograph of right now, and, in the future, no matter wherever you are or wherever I am, when we hear *Old Days* playing, we will always remember this moment in time." As predicted, the photo may have been eventually lost or discarded but the memory never was. *Old Days...*

Wednesday, July 28th
Jive Talkin' The Bee Gees

One winter out in Denver, Dollar Bill had been recruited by friends who were brokers in an over-the-counter penny stock company. A government sanctioned gambling operation, specializing in wildcat oil companies and IPOs, initial public offerings, both of which vehicles would at first shoot up in price and then go bust shortly thereafter. That October, at the urging of some of these broker buddies, Bill had taken one of those four-day, twelve-hours-a-day Securities and Exchange Commission cram courses and did in fact become a licensed SEC agent. Alas, the coming of spring put the job in clearer perspective, the upshot being that in order to become successful (like some of the millionaire brokers in the company) one needed to put in two or three years of mostly cold telephone canvassing and pestering friends that one already knew. With this bleak, exhaustive prospect on one hand and becoming "rich and famous" overnight on the lifeguard stand in Wildwood by the Sea, Bill went back for yet another summer.

This July afternoon at the beach, Dollar Bill took the opportunity to do a little social schooling with his rather shy rookie stand partner, Nick. Bill began by asking Nick, "Why don't you call more girls over to the stand and get something going with them?" Nick thought for a while and then replied, "Well, I'm not always sure of what to say.to them." Dollar Bill laughed and said, "It really doesn't matter what you say. It's just a matter of whether or not they like you. I'll give you a good example. Last year, out in Denver, a couple of the boys went to the National Western Stock Show and Rodeo. At the rodeo, we got really good seats. They were down low and my seat was right on the aisle. After a few beers, I began to compliment cowgirls on their cowboy hats as they walked up past me to their seats. Some of them, no doubt liked what they saw, and stooped down to say 'Hello.' After a while, fueled by the *Coors*, I began to say 'Nice hat' to girls who weren't even wearing one. And, guess what, some of them still stooped down to get acquainted. So, you see, Nick, it really doesn't matter what you say. If they like you they will be receptive to you no matter what."

After this bit of coaching, it wasn't too long before Nick was tossing out lines like, "Oh, you girls are back" to ladies whom he had never seen before. Or, having no idea where the ladies were from, he'd say, "You girls are from Delaware, right?" So, Dollar Bill was right. If the ladies were at all interested in you, saying any silly thing at all would bring them over to the lifeguard stand, and from there the real conversation would begin.

Thursday, July 29th

It had been almost a week since that whirlwind weekend with Stephanie and Hillary, and all that Alfie could think about was when they'd be back. What Alfie didn't know, or for that matter, did *anyone* else know, was that these two lovely ladies not only loved to fuck guys together, but that secretly they were lesbian lovers. Even back at the Manhattan offices, fellow workers hadn't the slightest suspicion that they were, in fact, "a couple."

In Staten Island, where they lived, they both kept separate apartments. If anything, friends and relatives thought that they were probably two lonely career girls who would get together at one or the other's apartment to watch some TV. Little did they know that the TV was rarely turned on. After having to submerge their feelings for each other all day at work, once alone again, they kissed like long-lost lovers, and spent most of their time naked together in bed, kissing, licking, and sucking, and, in general, relishing each other's body.

From time to time, so as not to get stale or to lose their appetite for men, they'd strap on a big rubber penis and go at it like they were boy and girl. Just like the ladies choose men to buy their next drink at a bar, they had zoned in on Alfie at the *Southwind Bar* that afternoon a few weeks ago in Wildwood. Spellbound as he was, Alfie hadn't given much thought to the fact that when the three of them were together in bed, and, in between his erections,

147

they did occasionally lick each other's pussies. He just thought, "This must be just a 'normal' part of the *ménage a trois.*" After all, who's to question such great, good fortune?

Friday, July 30th

Marcy, a very poised, eighteen-year-old brunette, who was to start nursing school in the fall, had come to *the Shore* from Conshohocken with her Aunt Marge, sister to Marcy's mother who had died when Mary was just ten. Aunt Marge had carried out her responsibility as though her deceased sister was watching and Marge was being graded. Although Marge kept a rather tight rein on Marcy, what harm could there be in a solitary walk on the beach. "I'll be back in an hour or so," Marcy had said. And, Marge went back to her 600-page novel.

Most guards are discouraged by bad weather, not Mick, who, on stand # 13 switched to his "strays" mode. In lifeguard slang, strays are females walking the beach alone. As Mick would say, "For some strange reason overcast skies bring out the strays." Strays fell into three general categories: girls who are not getting along with the girls that they came to *the Shore* with, solitary girls down with relatives, or, sometimes, a woman whose husband is not in town with them.

Married women are usually on vacation with the husband, but sometimes they do find themselves alone during the week when the spouse has had to return to work. Some of them can be persuaded to have a fling, whereas, others in this category are cougars looking for a young, handsome buck with whom to have a little extra-marital adventure. They might pretend that they have to be talked into it, but once they pick out the younger lifeguard it's a done deal.

In this vein, last year, Alfie had noticed a very attractive woman sitting on a beach blanket with a gentleman who appeared to be either her husband or boyfriend. True, she and Alfie had made eye contact a few times over that weekend, and, you might say she even flirted a bit with him. But, never a word was spoken between them, not even an overt "Hi." Come Monday, Alfie surmised that they had left. It had been a nice little flirtation, Alfie thought. Then around three that afternoon, the "wife" surprised Alfie by suddenly appearing right there next to the side of his stand. Without a word, she reached up and slapped the key to room 311 of the *Eden Roc Motel* on his thigh. Then, just as abruptly, she turned and left. Sitting up there on the lifeguard stand offered great advantages in meeting the opposite sex, but Alfie thought to himself, *This is ridiculously easy.* Stacy Ellison, at thirty-seven, had a body that would have rivaled any eighteen-year-old beach bunny, the product of a very cushy life and five-times-a-week workouts at her local spa and gym. Alfie did at first have some misgivings about her being married, but they dissolved when she told him, "Don't worry; I do this this kind of thing whenever I get a chance." They spent the next four nights together, before she kissed him goodbye and drove off home to Upper Saddle River, New Jersey. He had asked her, "Are you coming back down to *the Shore* again this summer?" But, the best she would offer was, "I don't know." And, with that, the tail lights of her BMW were that last Alfie saw of her.

Today, on *this* especially overcast day, with few bathers or walkers on the beach, lifeguard Mick had his 360-degree scan working and spotted Marcy some fifty yards off his stand. With a little chirp on his *Acme Thunder* whistle, he rather officiously called her to the stand, a maneuver that his fellow guards referred to as "the point." Approaching the stand meekly as though she had possibly done something wrong, she was pleasantly relieved when Mick's "Hello" broke into a big, broad smile. "Hi, I'm Mick. Where ya from?" "My name's Marcy and I'm from Conshohocken. "Oh, I'm from Pennsylvania, too. Chester, Pa.," Mick said. "We're down for five days," Marcy added. "Who is 'we'?" "Oh, my auntie and I." They chatted for over an hour and both were pleased for the company. Eventually, the conversation got around to, "What are you doing tonight?" "My auntie is pretty strict, so I don't think I'll be able to get out tonight." "How about just a harmless walk on the boardwalk?" said Mick, surprising himself, in that he meant it. 'Oh, I don't know, but I'll try." They tentatively arranged to meet on the *boards* at her street at seven.

Against her better judgment, Aunt Marge relented, agreeing to let Marcy take a walk on the boardwalk, "If you'll be home by nine." The rendezvous went as planned and before too long they were hand in hand, experiencing a warm glow between them. "I'm really happy that we could get together tonight," Mick told Marcy. Not accidentally, they came to Mick's street and he suggested that they stop by his place. Marcy diffidently said, "Ok, well just for a little while." She didn't drink but Mick did and had a beer, and then they talked some more. On his futon, he put his arm around Marcy and she snuggled closer. Then they kissed until it was nearing nine o'clock. Just that, just kissing. Glancing at her watch, Marcy said, "Mick, we'd better get going. It's almost nine, and Aunt Marge is pretty strict." They got up and Mick walked her to her street head on the *boards* and for the first time Marcy came to realize that you can have as much fun before nine as after nine. And, to Mick it brought to mind what he already knew, that a lifeguard has the rare opportunity of falling in love many times over a summer. Marcy enthusiastically agreed that she'd come visit Mick at his stand the next day. Then, she went home to auntie and Mick out to the bars.

Saturday, July 31st

On this day at the beach Alfie was imparting some of his beach wisdom to Jeff, saying, "The general public, beachgoers, that is, regularly have the mistaken notion that we as lifeguards like bad weather. They think that we like it when we have little or nothing to do. But, as you already know, lifeguards revel in fair weather. We like doing the job most when it's busy. In foul weather, time really drags on, with no bathers in the water. Also, our social life, girls, depends on good weather. With no walkers, no prospects.

151

"We did have a goofball, come to think of it, a few years ago who wore a tee-shirt on the life guard stand, the back of which read, 'Now that you've seen the beach, turn around a go home.' That only lasted until Cap saw it and made him take it off. Needless to say, with that sort of attitude that guy is now long-gone from the beach patrol."

Later in the day...

Given Harry's tutelage and "good" example," Steve was becoming more and more at home with the job, both the lifeguarding *and* with its social aspects. So much so that he began to feel comfortable with calling girls over to the stand and chatting with them. However, today wouldn't be such a good day for that. Unbeknownst to him, Lucy, his fiancée, had taken off work Friday, today, to drive down to *the Shore* and surprise him. Sizing up the situation on first setting foot on the beach from the boardwalk, her fury grew with each step closer to Steve, seeing him sitting up there on the wood, animatedly entertaining, what she saw as, "some beach bimbo." "Stephen, if this is the way you're going to act when I'm not around, then I'm not going to be around." And, with that she stormed off, leaving "Stephen" quite dumbfounded. Looking to Harry for solace and/or advice, Harry simply knowingly raised his eyebrows, no doubt, pleased with the "progress" that Steve was making. For the rest of the afternoon Steve rehearsed his apology for when he next talked to Lucy.

Harry knew the routine all too well. You get caught, then, make amends, promising to never do it

152

again. Then the cycle repeats itself. In the winter a lifeguard makes promises that, if he really thought about it, he couldn't keep. Too many summer distractions, beach honeys, that is, war against winter promises. "You know, Steve, early in the summer, in my second year on the wood, I had been caught red-handed by the winter girl. Afterward, she came to the stand in the next morning, before she was to head back to the city, and I was able to patch things up. Thinking myself in the clear, I was hand in hand with a hot new honey, walking along the very route that the winter girlfriend would have taken earlier on her way out of town. However, in getting caught up in conversation with her roommates, she had delayed her departure and saw me "cheating" again! Now, I had no room to wiggle out of it. Not long afterward, to my great relief, I became a free agent for the rest of the summer. It's just that variety presents too strong an argument against summer monogamy."

Later that night...

"But, Honey, I was just talking to that girl," Steve had rehearsed. Now, he had lots of quarters ready for the pay phone. He knew his story wouldn't be an easy one to sell to Lucy, his fiancée. He opened with, "Honey, when are you coming down again?" "Oh, so you can get rid of your beach bunnies before I get there, huh?" "No, no, no," Steve protested, although, in truth, he *had* lost some interest in persuading Lucy to come back down to *the Shore,* since having so much fun teaming up with Harry at night with girls from the beach. Somewhat relenting, "Maybe I'll come down this coming weekend," Lucy volunteered.

Saturday evening, July 31st

After last call at the *Spin-the-Wheel* at the *Southwind*, a half dozen of the boys got together on a porch at a lifeguard rooming house they called "*the Chateau.*" One of the brethren had overdone it at the *Southwind* and went to his room and passed out, one Walt the Salt. As the sun began its retreat for another day, Walt revived and was astonished to see the boys on the porch having some cold ones. Incredulously, he asked, "Aren't you guys working today?" A wink quickly spread and the spoof was on. "No, Walt, we're off today, but you better get going. It's 8:45 already." In a lather, Walt got his gear together and whisked off to "work." As he darted away they nearly wet themselves stifling the laughter. Walt must have really been confused as on his way to beach HQ it kept getting darker.

Book 4: August
Sunday, August 1ˢᵗ

Before going back-beach to the "head" at the hotel, Alfie took off his red top with the white WBP lettering, so as to not draw a potential complaint from local residents that the lifeguard was shirking his duty. By this time, rookie Jeff had a reasonable idea of what to look for and how to keep order, and could, therefore, be trusted to be alone on the stand for this short while. But, just to be sure and to keep Jeff on his toes he asked, "Are you going to be alright sitting alone while I go back beach." Jeff nodded and Alfie headed back beach.

On his way there, Alfie passed by a middle-aged guy on a blanket with a mammoth telephoto lens that sat on a small tripod. Given his suspicions, Alfie told one of the beach cops, "Hey, keep an eye on that 'photographer.' Just don't let him see you watching him." Afterward, the beach cop reported to Alfie, as expected, "Yeah, Alf, he goes into action every time you and Jeff call cuties over to the stand, and, especially when they have nice bodies and skimpy bikinis." Though not against the law, Alfie did resent it. And, so, told the beach cop, "Stay conspicuously close to this perv, and make him feel uncomfortable. This time, let him *know* that you're keeping an eye on him." Predictably, and not long afterward, the voyeur collected his belongings and, no doubt, found himself a more unsuspecting beach locale for his operation.

Time Has Come Today
The Chambers Brothers

As the summer days slipped carelessly by, Jeff would call Jan on more nights than not, while at the same time losing some of his interest in "the chase" for new romances. When it came to the point that they were together nearly every night, Jan summarily decided that Jeff was "the one." After all, in this day and age, she thought, "Nineteen is rather old to still be a virgin." It took several trips to the pharmacy, until there was a younger female clerk at the counter for her to ask, "Without a prescription, what would be the best way to not get pregnant?" Fortunately, the female clerk was so offhanded about it that Jan's embarrassment quickly faded, and she settled on a using diaphragm. Intimating her decision to Jeff, he went gently as could be and now their lovemaking was complete. Even with this big change, Jan continued to keep up her morning rule, telling Jeff, "I still want to get back to the apartment before the sun comes up, and to be able to shower and dress for chambermaiding with my other roommates." Jeff thought it a small price to pay for such delicious company.

Monday, August 1st

Over Marcy's remaining days in town Mick looked forward to her daily visits at the stand. Knowing that a lifeguards' talking time was restricted, she kept her visitations to just fifteen minutes or so. *There'd be lots of time tonight,* she thought. And, since Marcy had the immutable nine o'clock curfew, they added to their time together by meeting on the *boards* at six instead of seven. Progressively, their time on the boardwalk shortened, allowing more time for intimacy. In bed, Mick never pushed the matter, sensing how new all this was to Marcy. On their last night in bed together Mick eventually got down to only his jockey briefs and she her panties. Both of them still had the scent of the sun so pleasantly on their skin. They kissed passionately for hours as Mick deftly massaged her vulva through panties that had grown wet with excitement. Tentatively, and at Mick's gentle urging, she stroked his penis, taking her miles ahead of where she had ever been before.

On her last day, before leaving town with her unsuspecting auntie Marge, Marcy made her final stop by Mick's stand. After checking that the brass' Jeep was nowhere in sight, Mick sprung down and gave Marcy a hug and kiss to remember. Marcy said, "I really doubt that I will be able to get back down to the beach again this summer, but luckily," she said, "we won't be that far apart over the winter, with you in in Chester and me in West Philadelphia, in nursing school at Misericordia College. And, as you know, I'll be out from under Aunt Marge's watchful eye. As a first year nursing student I will still have a curfew, but it will be eleven o'clock on weekdays and one a.m. on weekends." And, most importantly, she would be less than a half-hour away from Mick. Without realizing it, Mick had found his winter girlfriend, and Marcy had discovered her first love.

She bade a tearful "goodbye" and said, "I wish Labor Day could come tomorrow."

Monday, August 2nd

"Oh, come on, Honey," Steve followed up his Saturday call with. "I know we'll have a good time when you get here. We can go out to dinner on Saturday night. There's a great seafood place that I know you'll love. So, let's just forget about what happened the last time you were down here. OK?" Lucy did soften and told Steve, "OK, I'll be down to *the Shore* this Saturday afternoon." But, sensing that Lucy may be setting a trap, and just to be on the safe side, Steve avoided having girls line up on his side of the stand, even if they were talking to Harry. And, with that, most of the fun went out of the job.

When Lucy did get to the beach that Saturday afternoon, Steve suspected that she had been there earlier, spying on him. Their relationship had surely changed. Steve didn't dare suggest that she *not* spend the day right behind their stand by using Harry's suggested tactic of saying that, "The bosses didn't like girlfriends at a guard's beach for the day." With the boys' operation shut down for Saturday and Sunday, and Harry having to act solo, Harry would just arch his eyebrows in an "I told you so" expression, to which at this stage, Steve could only silently accent. *Hurry up Monday.*

That first night, Lucy and Steve did go out to *Noel's Seafood House,* but he had trouble masking his boredom with the place. Sitting there making small talk and listening to the canned elevator music in the background, the tempo of Steve's summer had come to a virtual halt. Just two months ago, he would have enjoyed this sort of setting. But, Lieutenant Shelly had certainly been right in saying that in a few weeks on the wood a rookie wouldn't recognize himself in the mirror. This tedious dinner with Lucy brought it home to Steve just how much he *had* really changed. His free and easy life as a summer ocean lifeguard brought him to even resent, 'though quietly, Lucy's calling him "Stephen." The name was just too formal for the guy that he now saw himself as.

Monday night, Tuesday morning…

Clem threw the clock away on Monday night before his RDO, "regular day off" on Tuesday. In the bars, he kept saying, "Double OT, out tonight. off tomorrow." And, he kept throwing the beers back. At closing time he asked an "old reliable" of his, Linda, "Would you like to come back to my place and have some real fun." She did, and they did. In the early morning, she left in such a fury to be on time for work that she left her white lace panties behind. Half-asleep and lost in reverie, Clem followed his nose to the pillow under which they were semi-hidden. Reflexively, Clem pulled them over his head, aligning the fragrant crotch area of the panties with his nostrils. Sweet dreams. Dunes, his stand partner discovered him around nine, since they had arranged to go waterskiing that morning. "What the hell is this about, Clem?" Still groggy, Clem just laughed and said, "Oh, come on, Dunes, tell me you never do this."

Tuesday, August 3rd

The Slippery Rock University girls, Jan, Miriam, Betsy and Mary, were virtually down to a trio, now that Jan devoted most of her free time to Jeff. Luckily, Alfie had coached him, "Jeff, we don't want any girl hanging around the chair too long. So, why don't you tell Jan that the 'jeep,' that is, the bosses don't like lifeguards' girlfriends spending a lot of time at a guard's beach? Say that they think that the lifeguard would be too distracted." Jeff did as directed, and with this, Jan took the hint and only stopped by a time or two throughout the day to say "Hello." As lifeguards know, having a lifeguard's girlfriend, even if it's the other guard's girlfriend camped out behind their stand shuts down the operation and makes for a long, long day on the wood.

Of the remaining active trio, Betsy invariably took charge of the strategy to meet boys. By day, she'd say, "Girls, let's put our blankets here," which would be a spot that she chose because it was closest to a group of good-looking guys. At night, out at the bars, she would position the girls somewhere along the path to the bathrooms. "This way, the boys get to see you on the way in, get to think about what to say if they're interested in us, and they conveniently pass by us on way out. Then they don't have to overcome any shyness that they might have, in crossing the dance floor, just to say 'Hi.'" All in all, the girls were having a bang-up summer, with, perhaps, the exception of Mariam, who found more romance in novels than with the in-the-flesh variety. She often

160

thought to herself, *I don't know if this is really where I should be spending my summer. It's great for my roommates, but I'm not so sure it's for me.*

Wednesday, August 4th

Nick, on stand #6 with Dollar Bill, had heard lots of stories from the lifeguards who wintered in Colorado, and on this slow, overcast day he thought this a good time to get some background to these tales of winter fun. Nick had just finished up his four years at Temple University with a degree in education. He had done his student teaching at an inner-city middle school in Philadelphia, and he knew that teaching the reluctant wasn't for him. To seal the deal in nixing Philly as his choice of winter residence, his father had just retired, and after 35 years in the "City of Brotherly Love," his parents, Dot and Leo, had sold their house and were moving to a quiet little bayside retirement community, just seven miles across the South Jersey cape from Wildwood. Nick knew that he'd suffocate spending his winters there, so he was ripe for suggestions.

Collectively, the lifeguards represented a highly adventurous group. If a guy weren't particularly so when he had become a Wildwood lifeguard, the experience of having so much summer fun led the young man to expect life to continue being a great time. The guard's old home town paled in comparison to the faraway cities and towns of which the new guy had heard veteran lifeguards tell stories. Here were fresh new ideas bandied about on how to keep the party going. Visions of new places: Colorado, California, Hawaii, Costa Rica. Wow!

161

And, some of the guys the new kid was lifeguarding with this summer had actually been to these places, and spent their winters there. *Come to think of it,* Nick mused, *no one had ever mentioned any of these places back in the neighborhood.*

By now, nearly a dozen lifeguards spent their winters in Colorado. The majority of them liked Denver, with its lively nightlife, centered in Southeast Denver. A few of the boys worked the mountains, either teaching skiing or bartending. And, two of them found teaching positions in Colorado Springs. The beauty of the Colorado option was that the summer and winter seasons didn't exactly run one into the other. After the summer, there were a few months before one needed to get out west, time to enjoy the typically beautiful Indian-summer weather at the now-near-desolate beaches of South Jersey. Then, with the season ending around late March in the mountains, there was a month or so to head down to Mexico, to either Mazatlan or Puerto Vallarta, and to live on the cheap in either of these two beautiful beach-resort towns, towns where lots of California and Arizona coeds spent their spring breaks.

In this one afternoon, on stand #6 with Dollar Bill, Nick had fairly well made up his mind. He'd connect with a few of the guys when they began the trip west, set up in Denver with that nucleus of mates, and apply to substitute teach. This would give him a preliminary look at Colorado, and from there he'd be able to decide which part of Colorado would suit him best. How pleasant when such weighty matters could be settled so easily in one afternoon, at the beach and up on the lifeguard stand.

Back on the loose…

Marcy's departure threw Mick back into his every-night-out-at-the-bars routine, although now those nights out didn't seem as much fun. At the *Terminal Bar* one night Alfie had asked him, "What's with you, Mick? You don't seem like you're into it. Come on, my man, there's still a lot of summer left, and a lot of girls to meet. You gotta get back to being a Wildwood lifeguard." Alfie's goading did serve to wake Mick up a bit.

Thursday, August 5th
Back Home Again
John Denver

A sad day at the Greyhound Terminal. The experiment had failed. The remaining Slippery Rock girls, Jan, Betsy, and Mary were bidding a tearful good-bye to Miriam, at least until classes began again. It was the other three who had talked Miriam into going in with them on a place for the summer at *the Shore*. Collectively they thought it would bring her out of her shell and that she'd come to enjoy her time there. She had been a good sport about it all, though, tagging along at the others' insistence, but finally her homesickness won out. She missed all the familiar touchstones of home, her younger brother and sister, her comfortable bedroom, and breakfast and dinners with mom and dad. Wildwood, with all of its freedom just wasn't for everyone. Not for one moment on the long bus ride home did she give a second thought to her decision.

Friday, August 6th

Relieved to be back home in Conshohocken, Marcy's Aunt Marge settled back into her routine of gardening, reading, and playing bridge with her cohorts at the Daughters of the American Revolution lodge. When she looked back at their trip to the Jersey *Shore,* she felt pleased that she had raised such a well-behaved niece. The trip to *the Shore*, without being expressed to Marcy, was for her benefit, intended as a pleasant break from her candy-striping duties at their near-by hospital. At the bridge table she had told her good friends, "You know, even in my younger days I didn't have much of a taste for the seashore, although on this recent trip I did enjoy the break from city heat and the fresh ocean breezes." Marcy spent the rest of the summer in reverie of the dreamlike time she had had with Mick, and of those striking blue eyes and that smiling face of his.

We'll sleep in September!

Toward the end of every summer guards would be asked by summer friends, "Are you coming back next summer?" On most beach patrols guys would typically equivocate, with a "Maybe" or "I hope so," but for the most part that wasn't so with Wildwood Beach Patrol lifeguards. "You bet I'm coming back!" or, just, "Definitely!" would be the tone of their fairly universal reply. They just had to find ways of doing it. Teachers and students were in the clear for their returns. Other guards availed themselves of a number of *modi operandi*. Often as summer approached and their winter-job productivity began to slip they'd eventually say to the boss, "You can't fire me, I quit." Or, some would simply go to lunch one fine spring day and not return to work.

Summer lasts from 102 to 108 days, depending on when the Friday of Memorial Day weekend and Labor Day Monday fall. And, as summer wanes, the days become more and more precious. A few summers ago, Alfie and Dollar Bill were invited over to a barbeque at one of the guard's parents' house, and afterward passed out lying down side by side on a double bed in the family's spare bedroom. Some time went by before Alfie popped up, as if from the dead, and threw his arm across Bill's chest. Bill jolted upright when Alfie just about shouted, "Hey, what are we doing! We'll sleep in September." Ten minutes later they were out the door. Subsequently, throughout the years, "We'll sleep in September" has become the battle cry of Wildwood lifeguards as they inevitably begin to run out of summer days.

On the job training...

In Alfie's relatively short 11 years "on the beach" he had seen quite a few beach patrol ironies. Chief among this category were the histories of the captains of the adjacent beach patrols: to the north, North Wildwood, and to the south, Wildwood Crest. Since the appointment of a beach patrol captain falls to the whim of the politicians in power at the time, no official list of qualifications exists. To the north,

165

the captain at the time of this story was one, Captain Black, who did have a few years on the beach as a lifeguard, but over winters had to take a job as a clerk in a hardware store. Eventually, he found himself stuck there year round among the nuts and bolts, since he couldn't afford the pay-cut that returning to the beach would bring. That is, until the right pols won the vote and, over-night, hardware clerk Black became Captain Black of the North Wildwood Beach Patrol. And, to the captaincy he brought all that he had learned in the hardware store. Small-town magic. Actually, Captain Black was a slur nickname given him, owing to the fact that one of his first moves as captain was to change the traditional "red top" of his lifeguards' uniform, to black, probably the least visible color at any distance, and in effect, diminishing this essential aspect of communication from lifeguard to lifeguard during rescue actions.

To the south, with the Wildwood Crest hierarchy, a similar history ordained its present captain. Prior to Bud Hobson becoming its captain at twenty-three, the captain was Joe Freeland, who might be remembered from the story of how Seadog, Gary Lieber came to work WBP after being driven off the Wildwood Crest BP for getting "too old," at twenty-three. When Captain Freeland decided to call it quits, the average age of his guard compliment was nineteen, with an average number of years' experience at less than two years. When it fell to Freeland to nominate his successor, he chose a

166

"senior guard," Bud Hobson, who at the time had had a scant three years on the wood.

Among seasoned guards of the Wildwood Beach Patrol, conventional wisdom held that it took about four to five years to just to become a really fine lifeguard. Most of these guards would laughingly look back on their early years on the wood and say something to the effect of, "Yeah, in those first few years on the job I really thought I had it down, but, in retrospect, I didn't know my ass from my elbow about ocean lifeguarding."

So it was that at the helms, north and south of Wildwood by the Sea were captains with negligible experience. Whereas, in stark contrast, in the center of this six-mile island stood the Wildwood Beach Patrol, overseen by a captain with forty-plus years of experience, Captain Capacio. True, from one election year to another, he had had to humor the different personalities that changes at City Hall brought about, but in the end, his record had always supported his continued tenure. All in all, a jewel of a captain.

Friday, August 6th

As the summer rolled into August, the water became persistently rougher, due primarily to tropical storms and hurricanes brewing in the south Atlantic and working their way north along the eastern seaboard. With this change in the weather, the likelihood of ocean rescues went way up. Out in front of Alfie and his rookie Jeff were loads of bathers and to Alfie's trained eye all seemed to be under control. Nonetheless, Jeff thought that a young couple who were off by themselves might be having

167

a little difficulty, since the girl had the guy in a tight hold around his neck. Alfie put his binoculars on the couple and they appeared to quite gleeful, so he calmed Jeff, telling him that the couple was just "getting it on" in the water. Lifeguards, themselves, from time to time were known to take a honey out into the water to "get in there," and Alfie was sure that that was exactly what the couple was doing, that is, until a middle-aged gentleman came frantically running up to the guards' stand and screamed, "Those people are in trouble." With this, Alfie jumped down and rushed into the water to initiate the rescue. Jeff stayed momentarily behind, just long enough to send the whistle alert up and down the beach and then followed Alfie. In a matter of very few minutes, the two victims were being towed in to safety. Secretly, Alfie did feel a bit red-faced about the incident, but, his self-explanation was that he had interpreted the situation in light of the freewheeling seventies, and didn't want to come down on the couple's fun.

Sunday, August, 8th

When lifeguards were in the locker room, either before work and getting showered and ready to go out to the beach, or, while "doing weights" after beach hours in HQ, the boombox constantly put out music. *This* morning when WMMR, an Atlantic City radio station was playing the Rolling Stones *Satisfaction,* and the DJ came on afterward and said, 'Yeah, folks, that's a great one from 1963," one of the rookies turned to Alfie and said, "Yo, Alfie, that's a song from your time, right?" Alfie turned to

168

the newbie slowly and deliberately and said, "Listen, kid, *this* is my time." And, that was entirely true. Working the beach patrol sort of froze you in time, so that just as a lifeguard had had some rollicking fun while listening to *Satisfaction* back then, songs like Thin Lizzy's *The Boys Are Back in Town* now formed the background to this year's fun

As the days in August began to tumble off the calendar, "We'll sleep in September" became the mantra among the lifeguards of Wildwood. Just in case any of the guards were unaware of just how many precious days of summer were left, Alfie would announce the number at morning roll call, just after Captain Capacio finished his morning briefing and would ask, "Does anyone have anything to add?" Today, Alfie announced, "Fellas, there are only thirty days left in the summer. Be sure to make them all good ones." A cheer from the troops and they then headed down the ramp and out to their posts on the beach. Throughout the day, friends who were down for the summer would check with Alfie as they walked by his stand. "How many left today, Alf?" Alfie had brought many a beach-goer's attention to just how valuable each remaining day was. Almost like a preacher, he had sold them on his way of thinking.

Monday, August 9th

Today, with the beach packed to near-capacity, Rob and Brian were having a good laugh with two ladies with whom they were out with until the wee hours the night before, when suddenly Rob spotted the two cuties whom they had entertained

169

earlier the same night. Uh, oh! Fortunately, they were still two stands away. Hastily, Rob called down a guard from each of the adjacent stands to cover for them. As they launched the surfboat through the waves, there was still a hundred yards or more to spare, before the early dates would have run into the late dates. Standing on the stern seat, safely outside the breakers, Brian could see the late girls walking away from the lifeguard stand just as the early ones were about to arrive. From the distance of the boat to the beach, the whole business seemed to have taken place in slow motion. It worked so well, that the late shift girls didn't notice Rob and Brian waving to the recent arrivals to the stand. Simple beach mechanics.

Tuesday, August 10th
A Coney Island of the Mind
Lawrence Ferlinghetti

On summer nights, the two-mile by thirty yards wide boardwalk would be clogged with walkers from one end to the other. Along this span were five amusement piers, each jutting far out into the ocean. Rides like the Giant 156-foot Ferris wheel, roller coasters, and bumper cars, just to name a few. Dazzling lights whirled and carney shills were everywhere. Cries of "Knock the bottles down" or "Break the balloons" filled the air. Pizza and Philly cheese steak joints dotted the *boards* at short, frequent intervals. Even more prominent were the tee-shirt stalls, with shirts announcing, "I am a virgin (but this is a very old tee-shirt)" or "Good girls go to heaven, bad girls go the Wildwood by the Sea." And, of course, the classic in bad taste, the shirt pair that read, "Stupid" on the one and "I'm with Stupid," with the arrow pointing left or right, on the other.

From the look of most of the retail shops and stores on the *boards,* one might have guessed that they would attract a rather low-class crowd. Not that they weren't there, but many other types joined them, as well. Families vacationing in other beach resort towns from as far away as twenty-five miles were drawn to this nocturnal entertainment mecca. Folks staying in the more upscale beach resorts found that there was precious little to do at night outside of getting ice cream and pizza in their beach towns. Consequently, the two main north-south routes, the *Ocean Drive* and New Jersey Route 9, were jammed nightly with cars wending their way to the big boardwalk of Wildwood. Another group that would find their way to the boards were the families who opted for cheaper, much cheaper, lodging, and were staying out at the surrounding offshore camp grounds. Chief among this crowd were the French Canadians.

Younger Girl The Lovin' Spoonful

Perhaps a bit surprisingly, a total unrepresented sector of vacationers on the *boards* was lifeguards. With the drinking age in Wildwood at eighteen, the boards held little fascination to even the younger guards. That's why Captain Capacio, up on the boards to do a little fund-raising for the annual Wildwood Beach Patrol yearbook, thought it unusual to run into Jack and Dan mulling around the street head of Cresse Avenue on the boards. "Ah, Cap, we're just waiting around for some friends from

Philly, before going out to the bars." And, although not totally convinced, Cap left it at, "Well, have fun, fellas," and, "Not out too late," and was off on his business.

In truth, Jack and Dan, operating as Rob and Brian, had earlier that day on the beach set up dates with two Wilkes-Barre cuties. The coeds had, at 18, just graduated high school and were starting at King's College in the fall. Needless to say, at 25 and 27, the lads would not have passed muster with the parents, so, by pre-arrangement with the girls, Jack and Dan enlisted the assistance of two rookie lifeguards to pick up and deliver their dates. The rooks, if a bit mystified by the operation, gladly complied, happy to have been able to have earned a few brownie points with these senior lifeguards. But, then again, who knows, should these rookies stay on the beach patrol long enough perhaps they'll be doing the same thing in a few years.

Later that night…

Ryan, or simply "Dunes," from his *M.O.* of inviting girls for an evening stroll through the desolate, high dunes that are found on the south end of the island, was well-mannered and polite. 'Kind of the nice kid next-door. Tall and lanky, at six-foot-two, with summer-blond curly hair and striking blue-grey eyes. Tonight, equipped with a downy blanket and a bottle of *Mateus* wine, Dunes planned to introduce Colleen to this new form of open-air fun. This night would be a very special date, indeed. Just as the last faint light of day waned, to the east-southeast the full moon would rise over the ocean.

When Dunes had met Colleen on the beach in the afternoon, he had asked her, "Have you ever seen the full moon rise?" Her "No, I haven't," was quite common a response, since very rarely did he ever get a "Yes" to that question, since most folks have never witnesses or even heard about the rising of the full moon. He went on to explain, "It's nothing less than spectacular, a huge yellow-orange globe rising over the horizon of a pitch-black ocean. It's absolutely shocking the first time you see it. And, it looks like there'll be a clear night tonight, so there should be just perfect conditions."

Colleen happily accepted Dunes' invitation and he picked her up at eight. Arriving just before total darkness, Dunes found an ideally situated and disserted beach. On stepping onto the darkened beach, she had remarked, "Wow, I've never felt cold beach sand before." Down at the water's edge, they climbed up an unoccupied lifeguard stand, and were treated to one of nature's finest displays. Just as a setting sun over a wide expanse of water grows larger and larger as it descends toward and then "into" the water, so too, the moon does the same, only in reverse. The moon rises as a fiery glowing sphere, taking up a wide expance on the horizon. After this wondrous celestial show, Dunes found a remote spot back in the high dune grass where on the blanket he and Colleen got to know each other a little better over the bottle of Mateus. As hoped, the moon and the wine set a romantic tone for the couple for the rest of their night together.

Friday, August 13th
Get Out of My Dreams,
  Get into My Car   **Billy Ocean**
      Friday on the beach, Walt the Salt and Dollar
Bill had met a couple of "older" ladies, that is, older
for Wildwood; they were in their early-twenties. The
date was set for nine, since beforehand the ladies,
Helen and Barb from Allentown, Pa. wanted to go
out to dinner and then shop for souvenirs on the
boardwalk. This arrangement left some free time,
drinking time, that is, before nine rolled around. Walt
said, "Hey, Bill, I have an idea. Let's get a case of
beer and cruise up and down Pacific Avenue. I
haven't moved the car in over two weeks, and the old
girl could use a little activity." So, the plan was on.
      Although, as mentioned before, the climate
and sanctions against drinking back in 'seventy-six
were still rather loose, Walt had picked up these
wrap-around vinyl plastic labels that perfectly fit
around a twelve-ounce can of beer. They came in
several versions, and, perhaps to avoid trademark
infringement, they had names that were just off the
real thing, names like *Caca Cola, Orange Crash,* and
1-Up. As part of the spoof, Walt the Salt and Dollar
Bill would hoist their cans in "Hello" whenever they
would pass a cop either on foot or behind the wheel
of his patrol car. After spending so much time on the
beach of Wildwood, driving the two mile stretch of
Pacific Avenue gave them a completely different
perspective on the town.
      After a few beers, they'd pick out a couple or
a group of girls, Walt would slow down as he moved

174

toward the curb, and Bill, in a very polite voice would say, "Excuse me ladies, but…" Then, once he had their full attention, he'd say in a very firm, policeman-like voice, "Get in the car!" Then the lads would just break up laughing. Most girls would just take it as the joke that it was, and laugh, themselves. A few would get annoyed. Oh, well… And, some, believe it or not, would actually get in the car. Walt and Bill always got a laugh thinking back to the one and only time that when the lads demanded, "Get in the car!" a group of girls shot right back, "Get out of the car!"

When nine came around and they met their dates, the "older" ladies from Allentown, the first thing that they said was, "You guys been drinking?" "Naw, Dollar Bill responded, "we just had some driving to do."

Also, this evening afternoon…

As another weekend approached, with Lucy's impending return to see Steve getting closer, he began to rehearse his reception, "Hi Honey, it's really nice to see you again." She did say she'd come down on Saturday, but again he sensed a trap. If she got there on Friday and he was even talking to a girl, there'd certainly be an explosion. Nonetheless, he had met a stunner on the beach that Friday afternoon and the wheels in his mind began to spin. Calculating the soonest that she'd arrive, he thought, *Now, I know that Lucy gets done work at five and that with getting ready and then driving down in weekend Shore traffic, she couldn't possibly get here before*

175

eight. So, I'll take the chance and bring the beach honey over to my place right after the beach.

What he hadn't factored in was that Lucy had taken off work early, at three. At around six-thirty, just as he and the honey were getting into it, there came a rap, a very insistent rap, on the door. Luckily, the honey was totally cooperative, if a bit miffed, and went out the back window, while still hiking up her panties and skirt and buttoning up her blouse. Lucy, sensing that the delay in his unlocking the front door meant that Steve might have been up to some monkey business. So, once the door did open, she dashed right by Steve without even so much as, "Hi," and went right to the bedroom. There, she immediately bent over and put her nose right to the "wet spot." *Guilty as charged!* Without a word, she spun around and was out the door and back on the Garden State Parkway ten minutes later.

Rather than have been panicked at Lucy's abrupt departure, Steve surprised himself by feeling a bit relieved. Almost out loud, he thought to himself, *I wouldn't have thought it possible, but I have come around to Harry's way of thinking.* With this *coup de grace* to the engagement plans, Steve saw the remainder of the summer in a new light. And, his first step in the direction of this new freedom was to hurry over to the hotel where the honey that had gone out the window earlier was staying, patch matters up, and get the romance going again. Now, Steve *too* began to count the days remaining in summer with quite a different perspective. Before they were the days remaining

176

until he got back together with Lucy. Now, they were the precious days remaining to have fun.

Saturday, August 14th

Bobby on stand #1 loved sitting with Ferris, now the Trashman. Since it is typical that out of any two girls on the beach that the lifeguards call over to their stand, almost invariably, one of them will be better-looking than the other. With other lifeguard partners, they'll often alternate "shooting on" the better looking one, while the other partner does the "benefit." Next time he'll get first pick. But, on stand #1 Bobby always got his choice. Trashman was only too happy to hook up with the lesser of the two. He'd tell Bobby, "You know, Bobby, I can always find something I like in a girl," by which he meant "any" and "every" girl. Bobby would just shake his head and say, "You're a lucky man, Trashman*." What a great stand partner,* Bobby thought.

There were some drawbacks to sitting with a rookie, though. Just a few days ago, Bobby had Trashman stay up on the stand while he walked down into the water to get a better look at a potential rescue situation. Sure enough, there were two adult bathers who had been taken by the south drift into a deeper area of the gully. The girl began to grab her boyfriend around the neck, a sure sign of trouble. From the water, Bobby blew "shorts," the signal to initiate a rescue, to Ferris on their stand. Correctly, Ferris sent the rescue signal left and right to the adjacent lifeguards. What he failed to do was take his sweat pants and top off before leaving the stand. By his second porpoise dive he must have weighed three-hundred pounds, and that, embarrassingly, ended his participation in the rescue.

That night, out at the *Terminal Bar,* Alfie pulled up a stool next to the embarrassed Trashman. "Rough day, eh, kid?" "Yeah, it sure was," was all the rook could say. "Well, let me tell you, we've all had those screw-ups in our first year on the wood. In fact, on my first day ever on the stand, I showed up without either a hat or sunglasses. And, back then umbrellas and sunscreen were frowned upon by the lifeguards. The popular "suntan lotion" was a mixture of baby oil and iodine. Oil on the skin for eight hours out there in the sun, as we now know, was like the basting on an oven turkey. Well, on my first day as a lifeguard I got a wicked dose of sun poisoning. My eyes swelled shut and my lips looked like inflated balloons. It took four days on strong antihistamines before I looked human again and was able to return to work. So, kid, don't let a little thing like going in with your sweats on get you down. It's all part of the learning process."

Meanwhile, on the fringe of the guard group at the *Terminal,* a bedraggled pair, Walt the Salt and Clem the Clam sat. The two had been out late just about every night for over a solid week and were now running on fumes. They agreed that it was definitely time to get on Captain Capacio's "slow belt." Walt's concession to slowing down was, "If I'm not in the sack by 11 tonight, with or without a honey, I screwed up." Walt was even willing to break one of his cardinal rules, namely, "going home with the same girl two nights in a row is like going home with the *Philadelphia Inquirer."* Reluctantly, he said, "I'd even do a 'repeat' if it meant getting a decent night's sleep."

Sunday, August 15th

"Yeah, the beach patrol is really a wonderful place to work," Alfie was telling Jeff this fine afternoon. "Remember Lt. Shelly telling you rookies to go home and take a good look in the mirror, because in a very short time as a Wildwood lifeguard, you'll never see that guy again. Well, he was absolutely right. After a summer of ocean lifeguarding, parents often noticed that their boys had new airs of self-confidence and responsibility. Good changes. Working the beach does invariably change people, but not everyone for the better.

"In rare cases 'the beach' has brought out the worst in guys, or corrupted former good qualities," Alfie went on. "Some never got over having the party end, turning to either drugs or alcohol in an effort to keep the good times rolling. A few years ago we had a guy work the beach named Larry Blanco, who was probably the most charismatic guy to ever work WBP. Handsome, with blond hair and piercing blue eyes. In his senior year of high school he was first-team All-Catholic in both football *and* basketball, and this was in Philly, where the total enrollment in the all-boys Catholic high schools was around twenty thousand. Larry Bianco was a very special athlete, indeed.

Larry received scholarship offers from dozens of Division I schools, but settled on the University of Miami, where he got straight A's in

179

partying and bombed out in his first year. He did return to work the beach that summer and for a few after that. Eventually, Larry took to drugs and alcohol to get him through the boring Philadelphia winters and eventually went downhill in the process, no longer returning to the beach. A few of the Philly guys would run into him during winters and reported that was now just a shell of the star that he once had been. His wan smile now missed a few front teeth and he had become a complete bum, mooching off former friends when he had occasion to run into them. One can only speculate what life would have held for him had he *not* become an ocean lifeguard and had not had that Wildwood Beach Patrol experience.

Monday, August 16th

Most Wildwood lifeguards don't like wearing a watch because it does make the time drag on, by always knowing just what time it is. They might keep one in their ditty bag and look at it every hour or so, but Alfie always knew when it was quarter to three, since that's when the big *Sea Commander* sightseer boat made its turn for home, some two hundred yards offshore of Alfie's stand. The *Sea Commander* was a converted navy PT boat that probably saw action in the Second World War, but now was outfitted to carry over a hundred sight-seeing passengers.

Once a summer, the clientele onboard the *Sea Commander* dramatically changed. A few summers ago some of the guards were at the *Terminal Bar* and got to meet the captain of the *Sea Commander*.

Somehow or other the topic of conversation came around to the possibility of a "bare bottom," that is, a *naked*, cruise. Captain Alexander agreed and a deal was struck. The boat would be readied on an off-night, a Monday, for a four-hour cruise; however, on this sailing, the boat would stay a full mile offshore.

The days leading up to the *special* cruise always entailed some delicate recruiting. Before invitations were extended to female prospects, the full details of the trip had to be explained, namely, that once outside of public view, all clothes were to come off and that there would be plenty of sex, but the "sex" part was entirely up to the girl, it wasn't remotely compulsory. Invitations were given very judiciously, otherwise the whole escapade might come to grief should any of the ladies be shocked, or, worse, horrified by the goings-on aboard the *Sea Commander* that night.

Without fail, year after year, thirty or so Wildwood lifeguards were able to gather the "just-right" group of female participants for the fun. With the night being a BYOB, "bring your own booze," this year it wouldn't be long before everyone was in the mood for this exceptional dispensation of all sexual morays. Girls who, no doubt, had the sexual fantasy of being done by more than one guy would have their pick of which lifeguard would be next. And, others who had boyfriends back home who never licked them would get to have that joyfully experience. All in all, sexual exuberance would rule the night.

Alfie looked around at the "chicks" that were boarding on this warm August night and said to Seadog, "I don't know if it's the tans, the shoulders with those white bikini lines, or the seashore air, but they all look so hot!" He couldn't stop thinking, *In a few minutes there all gonna be naked. Wow!* "You know, Seadog, just how lucky we are to be able to get to experience something like this? If half the guys who failed the lifeguard swim test because the water was too cold could have seen this, they probably would have toughed it out and passed the test."

Just as the boat pushed off the first rule of conduct was broken. The shy guy who showed up for the lifeguard test just two months ago, one Ferris Wooding, now Trashman, dashed to the very front of the *Commander* and literally ripped off his clothes, standing there at the bow like a Viking, exhorting his followers into action. "To the naked cruise," he loudly yelled, over the splash of the bow waves below. Murmurs of, "Oh, my God..." could be heard coming from the shocked dinners at the adjacent dockside restaurant. In just a few minutes away from the quay, darkness and distance veiled the revelers. Shorts and tops were everywhere strewn on the *Commander's* deck.

This was probably Alfie's ninth or tenth bare-bottom cruise and as he walked from stern to bow, checking out the doings, he had to almost say out loud to himself, *This is really fucking amazing.* There was Clem the Clam in his glory, licking a gorgeous, big-titted blonde, while she was sucking

182

on Dunes' dick. Through the window of the helm shed, Alfie peered in and saw Dollar Bill getting really creative. He was hanging upside down from an overhead pipe, while getting sucked off by a naked, fulsome brunette, all the while returning the favor, with his face buried in her crease. Walt the Salt called over to Alfie, "Hey, Alf, this is Debbie. Debbie, this is Alfie." Debbie momentarily paused the blow job and gleefully said, "Nice to meet you," Walt took this opportunity to refresh Debbie's drink, mixing her rum and coke with his phallus, to which she gave her smiling consent. "Yum, yum," she purred.

Half way to the bow, Alfie noticed Sandy, who was one particularly hot blonde, with a body that, in clothes, made your knees weak. Naked, she was breathtaking. Every guy on board wanted Sandy. And she was just as anxious to have them. Later that night, when back on dry land and over a few beers at the *Terminal Bar* Alfie confided in his stand partner, Jeff, "When I looked over I saw a few guys in line waiting to be next with Sandy, while at the same time I see a guy fucking her and she's giving another guy a blow job, think about it, we're on a boat full of naked chicks, and there's a line behind Sandy. She's just that hot!" But, with the selection process on the beach having gone on for a few days leading up to the cruise, there were loads of great-looking, sexy babes on the boat, romping around all naked and the majority of them into having sex with the boys. In a short pause from the festivities, Walt and Alfie were having a beer at the ship's rail, gazing at the nearly-full, gibbous moon's bright reflected swath on the blackened ocean when Afie looked at Walt and said, "You know, Walt, this is the kind of night that no one aboard this boat tonight will ever forget."

Monday, August 16th

Now with Steve's former fiancée, Lucy, out of the picture, Harry had in Steve a true stand partner, one with whom he could freely set up dates with good-looking pairs of honeys that they would chat up at the beach. Since Harry knew that Steve was still a bit "green" when it came to women, he thought that he's give him a little schooling on these matters, introducing Steve to the popularly held Wildwood lifeguard notion that goes, "Once you got a girl wet, she then thought like you did about sex." Or, another paraphrase of this was, "It was up to us (the guys) to trick them (the girls) into having a good time." The latter saying came from a story that a few of the lifeguards who spent their winters out in Denver told. Dollar Bill's rendition of it was, "There was this fellow, Freddy, who was a bit slow-witted, but a pleasant guy all the same. From time to time, we'd bring him along for a night's outing. After one such occasion, he was overheard telling some other friends that we had tricked him into having a good time." Harry went on to add, "Lots of girls *were* like that. They'd be ever so reluctant to let themselves go in the bed, but then after you get them wet, and they take off the brakes, the next day they'd be down at the lifeguard stand gushing about what a great time

184

they had 'last night.' And, saying, 'I'm not usually like that.'"

Tuesday, August 17th

Today the weather report called for "rain all day," which came as a relief to most of the lads of the beach patrol who had been out to sea last night on the *Commander*. In fact, it rained so hard in the morning during what would be set-up time that Captain Capacio held the boys back at beach headquarters, and patrolled the water's edge with two roving jeeps, manned with three or four lifeguards, enough should a rescue become necessary. From time to time during the first few hours of the morning there were breaks in the downpour, allowing the lifeguards to leave the headquarters and to go up to the boardwalk to get a bite to eat and to hang around the benches on the *boards* to people-watch.

Alfie enlivened the morning when he went to his locker and cut off an eight-foot length of string and to it he attached a dollar bill. From under the *boards,* he pushed the dollar up through a space between planks. Up on the boardwalk his accomplice, his stand partner, Jeff, would fix the dollar bill in place. Having heard what was going on up on the *boards*, just about every Wildwood lifeguard found a spot up there on the benches, a good vantage from which to catch the merriment. As Alfie would see the footsteps of the unsuspecting boardwalk stroller approach, he would pull the string a few inches, invariably piquing the unsuspecting dupe's interest, no doubt thinking the wind had

185

moved it. When the mark would bend over to pick up the dollar, it would disappear through the slit, sending a roar of laughter from the audience. More often than not, the momentarily embarrassed participant quickly saw the humor in the ruse and laughed along with the assembled corps of lifeguards.

The joke went afoul, however, when one enterprising lifeguard borrowed an nearly-empty mustard squeeze-bottle from a nearby hotdog stand, cleaned it out, and then, after filling it with water, he would squirt the water up through the planks' opening, soaking the spoof's bent-over victim. Needless to say, the water-enhanced trick nearly came to fisticuffs, bringing an end to the fun. But, it did pass an hour or so on this otherwise dismal beach day.

Under the Boardwalk
The Drifters

There exist some stories that have floated around lifeguard circles for so long that they have become legends, no one can be sure whether they really happened or they were invented, like some campfire story created to mystify neophytes. One that went back to nineteen seventy-six involved a certain girl, who became nicknamed, "Jaws," after that movie came out. This happened one rainy day on the beach when it wasn't raining hard enough to send the lifeguards back to the hotels for shelter, but persistently enough that there were virtually no beachgoers left on the beach.

From stand #11, Seadog noticed that at ten-minute or so intervals, the jeep that the driver and the lieutenant were in kept ushering a different pair of guards back toward the boardwalk. Strangely, though, the jeep didn't move toward a street head, where there would be off-beach access. Instead, the jeep would park and stay under the boardwalk. After watching this happen seven or eight times, Seadog blew a non-emergency signal for the jeep. After an abnormal delay, the jeep did arrive at lifeguard stand # 11. "Hey, get me in on this," Seadog said. The jeep guys laughed a little, called for a lifeguard to cover # 11, and whisked Seadog and Charley off to the *boards.* Seadog's suspicions were correct. But, when they got there, *Jaws* said she couldn't give any more guys the oral treatment. Her reason, after already sucking off and swallowing sixteen or so lifeguards, was, "I have to go to lunch." Seadog protested, "Aw, come on, just two more." "Alright, just you two guys, but then I really *do* have to go to lunch."

Wednesday, August 18ᵗʰ
Never Can Say Goodbye
  The Jackson 5
        One might surmise that the summer came to an abrupt ending with Labor Day Monday, however, the unwinding really began about two week before that, when families turned their attention to getting back to school. The effect was noticeable on the beach, with crowds being conspicuously lighter. Seasoned lifeguards saw this as the harbinger of summer's sad, but inevitable ending. A few of the guards, those who were teachers west of the

Mississippi, where schools started up *before* Labor Day, had to head west around the middle of August. Out west they don't pay much attention to Labor Day. Maybe it's bigger on the east coast where workers tend to be more unionized and the worker held in higher regard.

Gary Lieber, aka, Seadog, who coached a high-powered swim team on Maui, was in this group. Gary had a peculiar way of leaving, one that had notoriously become his trademark. He would keep the actual departure date to himself. Then, one day Wildwood lifeguards would begin to ask, "Where the hell is Seadog?" and it would slowly become evident that he had been up to his old tricks. *There* was a man who just didn't like "goodbyes."

During the summer, Seadog had a similar habit. When he had had enough on a given night out at the bars, he would just disappear. If he had to, he would feign a trip to the men's room and then just duck out. His reasoning was that he didn't want to hear, "Oh, come on, stay for just one more. It's still early." With no "Goodbyes," there'd be no need for an excuse for exiting.

Thursday, August 19th
Shark alert...

Bathers do lose all sorts of belongings in the ocean, from money to room keys. Alfie once discovered four twenty-dollar bills drifting around in ankle-deep water. Earlier this morning a complete set of upper dentures were turned in to Lt. Shelly and his jeep driver, Thomas, aka. "Moonman," which they intended to safeguard until their next trip back to

HQ. A bit later in the morning, more toward noon, the "jeep" noticed a large crowd gathered at the waters' edge. Shelly asked Thomas to work his way through the mob and check out what was going on. Apparently, a three-foot sand shark had washed up dead and a teenage boy, not being entirely convinced, was beating the carcass with a whiffle ball bat. Little did he and many of the others know, that the shark, instead having sharp teeth, had but a cartilage plate for "teeth." Thomas easily dispersed the people by simply grabbing the shark by the tail and removing it.

Once back at the jeep, he threw the shark on the jeep's wet-bed. Only a few yards away from the scene Thomas ran an idea past Shelly. Shelly gave his assent, and the dentures were jammed into the mouth of the shark, after which the conspirators drove the jeep slowly enough that bathers, by now a large group of them, trailed behind the jeep, marveling at what big teeth the shark had. "Wow, look at the teeth on that shark!" beachgoers would gasp. The boys drove the jeep like this until they could no longer suppress their laughter.

"Are you guys hungry?"

Having had so much fun with the shark's teeth, and in such a jolly mood, the lads devised another prank. In the bag that had held their morning donuts, they put the dentures. Sequentially, down the beach they drove, stopping at several lifeguard stands, saying to each pair of guards, "We had a few jelly donuts that we couldn't finish. Would you guys want them?" "Sure," invariably came the answer.

189

The ravenous lifeguards would reach into the bag. But, when they made contact with the false teeth and recognized what they were, *"Ah!"* the shocked lifeguard would loudly gasp and almost jump off the stand in revulsion. *For this, revenge would definitely be in order.*

Sunday, August 22nd
Rocky Mountain High
  John Denver

Last year, Tommy High, the beach cop turned lifeguard had been influenced to head out west with the Colorado contingent for the good life out in Denver. From year to year, the group varied in numbers from a half to a dozen or so guys, many of whom stayed at an apartment complex in southeast Denver, the social epicenter of Denver. The groups split up in to threes, taking nine-month leases on three-bedroom apartments. *Perfect!* The complex, the *Coronado Club,* had indoor and outdoor pools, tennis and basketball courts, saunas, and its own friendly bar. So, migration west was like taking a vacation from a vacation--the Jersey *Shore* in the summer and Colorado in the winter. When divided among three, their share of the rent on the three-bedroom apartment was nominal. Tommy High fit right in with the boys' every weekday happy-hour routine. Back then just about every bar and/or restaurant offered happy-hour, half-priced drinks, accompanied by free buffets, imagine that, all-you-want-to-eat food that ranged from fresh-cut prime rib, Alaskan king crab legs, to Gulf shrimp. The boys often battled snowstorms to make it to happy hours.

On one occasion, a group of the guys went to *McNichols Arena* to watch the Denver Nuggets play. In a veritable snowstorm on the way back on I-25 the heater/defroster quit, casting a fog on the inner windshield. So, resourceful men that they were, they began to spray de-icer, which had a strong ether-like smell, on the *inside* of the windshield. Along with keeping the inner glass clean, the vapors made the lads quite red-faced and giddy. Upon finally arriving at their favorite hangout, the very popular southeast Denver tavern, the *Bull & Bush*, the first girls that they met asked them, "Do you guys work in a hospital?" To which, the boys answered, "Yeah, we're brain surgeons," and broke out laughing hysterically.

Tommy High, the beach cop turned lifeguard, had been a sort of kick-around guy after high school, spending his winters at odd jobs in and around Cherry Hill, New Jersey. There, he had no credit cards but did have a checking account with a perpetual balance of zero. In Denver he came to learn that just about every transaction could be accomplished by writing a check on his newly opened Colorado bank account. When hearing of Tommy's checking account acquisition, and, knowing how Tommy was, Rob and Brian, who were Colorado winter regulars, told him, "Tear up the checkbook, Tommy, or else you'll never be able to come back to Colorado." And, right they were. When that spring came around, any number of establishments, from supermarkets to bars to liquor stores were looking for Tommy High. Bouncing checks in Colorado borders on being a felony. Now, this year, as the beach patrol job began to come to a close, Tommy High began to dread being faced with spending another awful winter, again, in Cherry Hill, New Jersey.

Teach Your Children
Crosby, Stills, Nash, and Young

After leaving the beach, some old guards come back for vacations with their families, whereas, others never are seen again. In either case, this largely depends on the girl they marry. Some domineering wives think that Wildwood just isn't classy enough for their tastes, and they have their family spend summer vacations in trendier, more upscale beach towns, like Avalon, Stone Harbor, or Sea Isle City.

With the guys who do keep contact with the Wildwood Beach Patrol, either by simply vacationing and beaching it in Wildwood or by showing up every year for the annual alumni weekend, there routinely is evidence of a rare phenomenon, referred to as *the lifeguard curse,* to wit, former lifeguards inexplicably have a greatly disproportionate percentage of daughters over sons. And, as might be predicted, these present-day fathers typically admonish their female progeny, "Stay away from the lifeguards," no doubt remembering their own repertoire of tricks for getting a girl into bed. Hypocritical behavior, no doubt, on the part of the old lifeguard, but probably safe advice, nonetheless.

192

Book 5: Early September
Summer's Almost Gone
   The Doors

True to form, the ocean began to get progressively rougher in August and then into September. Now, in their last full week of lifeguarding, the lads had been run ragged, with rescues and cover-ups going off in every direction, up and down the beach. Early lifeguard departures had added to the situation, thinning out the corps. "Days off" had been canceled a few weeks ago. At times throughout these difficult days, beaches had to be temporarily closed for fear of leaving them unprotected. Everyone knew that these times were coming, and for the first time this summer the lads would take Captain Capacio's advice to heart about getting on the "slow belt" on their remaining nights out after work.

That is, except for Rob and Brian who really felt that they were running out of time and were sprinting down the homestretch of summer. Tonight they had made the rounds, closing the *Fairview* at two and then heading north to Angelsea, for a few bars that were open until five a.m. By now, they were really showing the wear, with scruffy tee shirts and tangled hair.

Sometime around four a.m., finally on their way home, Rob stopped their beaten-up old Chevy Nova for a red light and in the pause, fell asleep at the wheel. Brian had dozed off a few blocks before. Without realizing it, the car began to creep through the intersection.   With the officer's rap on the window, Rob bolted upright and rolled down the window. Officer Romeaux knew the guards from the summer softball league, and gave them a break, saying, "Just park the car in that open lot over there, just across the street." Too tired to devise a way home on foot after parking the car at this late hour, the lads continued their slumber in their now-safely parked car. Just before dawn, another tap came, this time it seemed to be a vagrant at the window. With some annoyance, Brian rolled down the window slightly and looked questioningly at the bedraggled creature, who sheepishly asked, "Do you mind if I grab the back seat?" Rob turned to Brian, who by this time was awake, too, and said, "Man, do we look *that* bad?"

Saturday, September 4th
"Parting is such sweet sorrow."
  William Shakespeare
      The weather didn't quite cooperate this Labor Day weekend, with mostly cloudy skies and intermittent showers on both Saturday and Sunday. By midday Sunday, most tourists had forsaken hope of a day at the beach and were packing up and heading back home. All too late to rescue the weekend, the sun broke gloriously on Monday morning, giving the lifeguards of the Wildwood Beach Patrol a postcard day to remember.

      A few beach regulars, like Misses B. and then "Old Charley" came by to say goodbye for another season. Both of them knew just about every lifeguard who had ever worked the beach in the last thirty or so years. Over all those years, Misses B. rarely missed her daily workout, walking the two-mile beach of Wildwood end to end and back, while stopping by to say "Hello" to her favorites. She had married a lifeguard, who then became a doctor, and they had a son who lifeguarded throughout his college years, and, now, she had a grandson, Todd, the rover who was just a rookie. Old Charley walked the beach far less deliberately. His was more a visit "with the boys" to stop and chat and to offer his pals a measure of his "special cough medicine," in the form of a pint of apricot brandy. Misses B. and Old Charley were beach institutions, as much a part of the beach as seagulls and sand. A sad day it would be if either of them were to fade away one day.

Labor Day Monday, September 6th

And, so, the saddest, most dreaded day of the summer had ineluctably come, and in the last few hours of the day "on the wood," Alfie found himself lost in reverie of all the wild and funny things that had happened this summer, the summer of 'seventy-six. After the final knock-off whistle came down the beach and Alfie pulled his stand back for the last time this summer, he began his long introspective walk back to beach headquarters, and along the way he thought to himself, *You know, one of these days I ought to write a book about this wild summer.*

Tuesday, September 7th, 1976

As though nature had observed holidays, on the now nearly-desolate beach, thousands of seagulls had massed, awaiting the next "bird play." With scant few bathers in the ocean, striped bass had taken possession of the innermost gully, at only ten yards or so off the dry sand, and were chasing up minnows that were skipping out of the water trying to evade their doom. Once the minnows broke water, the gulls took flight and gorged themselves on the unfortunates, and a riot of squawking took over, emphatically punctuating another glorious summer.

The days after Labor Day Weekend:

Tommy High, the beach cop turned shaky lifeguard, whose bounced checks had forever banished him from Colorado, was driving a cab in Cherry Hill, New Jersey.

The other Tommy, the lifeguard, had come through another summer without "bringing anything home" to his winter girlfriend, Alison.

Disappointingly, Mick got home to find that Marcy had already been dating an intern. He mused to himself, *I hope the guy appreciates driving on the road that I paved.*

At last report, Johnny, the *Paperboy* was enmeshed in an acrimonious battle with his two siblings over the deceased father's will. The two had had nothing whatsoever to do with the old man for over 20 years, but surfaced like serpents from the grass while the death notice in the newspaper was but a day old.

Ferris, er, Trashman was back home with a *Rolodex®* of rather unattractive girls' phone numbers, ladies who would be more-than-happy for the attention.

Gary Lieber, Seadog, was back in Maui, keeping it to himself just how superior the beaches of the Jersey *Shore* had been. Sure, Hawai'ian waters may be more beautiful to the eye but for fun right off

197

the dry sand and into the ocean, Seadog knew the South Jersey *Shore* was better.

Peter O'Neill was biding his time until he got the call from the ski patrol out in Steamboat, Colorado. Until then, he was enjoying the terrific Indian summer beach weather and hoisting a few with long-time friends in the taverns of Cape May.

Lucy wouldn't return Steve's calls, so it looked like that was over. Steve, though, did have more than a few prospects for "winter girlfriends."

Jim McAlister went back to teaching in Massachusetts, with a whole new perspective. He had shaken the cobwebs that had ensnared him from those eleven years in the monastery and now after three full summers "on the wood" he had developed into the convivial, outgoing guy that now suited him so well.

Alfie's was back in the classroom, teaching juniors and seniors' math. His prospects of seeing Stephanie in the fall had faded along with his tan. Living and teaching just outside of Philadelphia, he had called and talked to Stephanie a few times, but she had just put him off. He had hoped to rendezvous with her, perhaps up in New York or Staten Island, but finally she told him that, "I become a different person in the summer when I cross that causeway bridge into Wildwood, so it wouldn't really work out, our getting together after the summer."

Rob, the Osprey, and Brian were on the beach in Cape May, right in front of the *Rusty Nail Tavern,* enjoying gin and tonics, where they planned to stay until word came of the first snowfall in the Colorado Rockies.

Likewise, Bill Hennessy, aka, Dollar Bill was in no hurry to get back to Colorado, rather, he planned to enjoy what can often be the best beach month of the year in South Jersey-- September.

For Clem, the Clam and Ryan, Dunes there was no rush to get back to lifeguarding in South Florida, since, in all aspects, the job there paled in beach action and social life, when compared to the summer that they had just had.

Charley Booth had started his freshman year at the Penn State Ambler campus, this time he'd be a college freshman *for real.* (Years later, when the *Martinique Lounge,* recall, the bar where at seventeen he had hooked up with lots of "older ladies," was condemned to the wrecking ball, Charley brought his beach chair and a twelve-pack of beer and reverently sat there and reminisced. When his wife discovered where he was, she went there and asked him, "Charley, what on earth are you doing?" He ruefully shook his head and said, "Honey, you just wouldn't understand.")

And, you can bet that no matter wherever these summer lifeguards of the Wildwood Beach

Patrol found themselves in the interim, none of them could wait until Memorial Day came around again.

About the Author

Mick Fee "sat the wood" for thirty summers as a South Jersey ocean lifeguard, taking in the four decades of the 60s, 70s, 80s, and the 90s. He now lives in Waikiki, on Oahu, in Hawai'i.

Acknowledgements:
What follows is a list of all the great guys, the lifeguards with whom I had the great good-fortune of having known and "worked the beach" with in the 60s and 70s. All of us owe a special debt of gratitude to the man, Captain John Capacio, who shaped us into proficient ocean lifeguards, and at the same time, gave us the latitude to have some wild summers. Also, special thanks to my lifeguard buddies, Joe Sindoni, who kept after me to make this book better and better, and to Steve Heatherington and long-time colleague, Jeffery Hall for their helpful advice.
Here is the crew, fellow lifeguards and good friends from *the 60s and 70s:*
Captain John Capacio, Joe Sindoni, Pete "Gull" Salo, Billy "Robo" Rowe, Billy O'Ware, Steve Hearherington, Tommy Dooner, Jerry Sieber, Rickie Grimaldi, Bobby "Loveman" Love, Eugene "Euge" Reidy, Jim "Snuffy" Singer, Charlie LaBarr, Michael "Marquis de la Plaige" Coogan, Larry "Laredo" White, Dale Hummel, Mike "Rego" Regosch, Johnny Ebert, "Johnny Mac" McAnany, Tom "Jelly Donut" Mooney, Billy Kindle, Billy Dobbins, Jimmy "Oakie" O'Kane, Sam "Bobo" O'Kane, Mark Aubin, Johnny Calabro, Ray and "Babe" Pashuck, Bobby Ott, Dennis Hart, "Dancin Dick" Chelekis, Joe Kelly, "Jimmy Mac" McManus, Michael "Meat" McManus, Dougie and Janet Ford, Dennis "Casper" Regan, "Robbie On the Rocks" Innes, Butchie "Zeus" and Billy Harris, Bert Soden, "Billy Jack" Gunther, Sammy Freas, Newt Hill, Eddie Spause,

Eddie Cahill, Rick "the Grec" Greco, Tommy and Mark Robibnson, Kenny Saup, Larry Ingram, Tommy Gavin, Tommy "Piez" Pietrzak, Ronnie Ianeri, Joe Cunningham, Rich Renza, Walt Lion, Michael Benson, Junebug, Stanley Byrne, Bob Fish, Billy Fox, George Croyden, Crazy Walt, Joe "Rocketman" Surrick, Johnny Gunther, Eloit Giacobello, Chuckie Reed, Denny Craft, "Moose" Kelly, Jack Downey, Lou Stopper, Neil Howett, Bob Gavin, Tom McFaul, Lew Ostrander, Bob Noone, Sean Ford, Billy and Teddy Phelps, the Mullin boys; Jimmy, Mark, and Danny, Skip O'Neill, Lou DeSimone, Peter "Rock" Ferrero, Reynolds Chanberlin, Owen DiLouie, "Rank Hank" Sibalski, Peter Hudak, Bob Stancavage, Paul Fuentes, John O'Brien, Ned Barnes, John and Sam Sposata , Joe Carroll, Nick Catanoso, Jimmy and Guy "Rockin' Robin" Celetti, Cliff Baldwin, Ed and Allen Szyszko, Bob Murray, John Peck, Tommy Griffin, John Dill,   Bobby Morris, Paul Toufel, Butch Cunningham, Herb Treffierson, John Teofilac, Jimmy Fee, Greg Sippa, Chuckie Patterson, Joe Lieberkowski, Linda Kelly, Franny , Mark, and John Zarich, Marc Camillo, John Dill, Bubby Hayward, Jimmy Nawn , John MacLennon, Mike Perna, George and Debbie Algard, Tom Mohan

Chair
| ***Number*** | ***Lifeguards (years of experience)*** |

1 Bobby Morrison, 11years, & rookie, Ferris,
      aka, "Trashman" Wooding

2 Larry Baxter, 4 years, & Jim McAllister,
      3 years

3 Walter Finley, aka, "Walt the Salt,"
      7 years, & Sam, 5 years

4 Harry Alston, 8 years & rookie Steve
      Murray

5 Tommy Timmons, 8 years & George,
      2 years

6 Bill Hennessy, aka, "Dollar Bill," 9 years
      & rookie, Nick Avalone

7 Alfie Henderson, 11yrs & rookie Jeff
      Connor

8 Rob, "Osprey," 7 years & Brian, 6 years
      (who are really Jack Innes & Dan Smith)

9 Clem, "the Clam" Harris, 10 years & Ryan
      "Dunes" Donovan , 7 years

10 Peter O'Neill, 9 years, & Stan Elkington
      , 4 years

11 Jerry Lieber, "Seadog," 11 years, &
      Charley Booth, 2 years

12 "Tommy High" Lane, 2 years & "Crazy
      Mike" McMasters, 5 years

13 Rick Stevenson, 8 years & Mick Noone, 5
      years

Rovers: Todd Collins, 4 years & Rookie Phil
      Forster

Captain John Capacio & Lieutenant Joe Shelly

Made in the USA
Lexington, KY
15 May 2014